FAIRY TALE LUST

FAIRY TALE LUST

EROTIC FANTASIES FOR WOMEN

EDITED BY
KRISTINA WRIGHT

CLEIS
PRESS

Published in the United States by Cleis Press Inc., 2246 Sixth Street, Berkeley, California 94710.

Printed in the United States.
Cover design: Scott Idleman
Cover photograph: Markus Amon/Getty Images
Text design: Frank Wiedemann
Cleis Press logo art: Juana Alicia

ISBN-13: 978-1-61664-615-8

Contents

FOREWORD

Angela Knight

When I was a child, I loved fairy tales. Evil witches, beautiful princesses, handsome princes—those tales of magic and romance captured my innocent imagination. As an adult, I learned that there was a distinctly dark edge to the original fairy tales that had been carefully sanitized out of the versions I'd read. For example, did you know that Sleeping Beauty in the original version woke up pregnant? Apparently her handsome prince did rather more than kiss her.

As for "Little Red Riding Hood and the Big Bad Cross-Dressing Wolf"—well, the kink factor in that one is obvious.

Fairy Tale Lust: Erotic Fantasies for Women explores the sensual potential in the stories we all heard as children, giving them the kinky edge I always suspected lurked under the surface. You'll find beauties, beasts, mermaids and handsome heroes aplenty here, along with enough deliciously sexy action to make your heart beat faster.

But what is it about fairy tales that makes us want to give

them a sensual twist? Maybe it's because when you go back and read them with adult eyes, the sexuality is already there. I wrote my own kinky version of the "Beauty and the Beast" story years ago, because I was so fascinated by the idea of falling in love with a beast.

Now, I loved the Disney version of that story—but am I the only one who wondered if Belle felt cheated when her raging Alpha Beast became a handsome Beta male?

Personally, I liked him better with fur, claws and a bad attitude.

Which brings up an interesting point. We know that as strong, intelligent, independent women, we're not supposed to want to be rescued by the handsome prince. We're not supposed to want the Beast.

Yet down deep in our secret hearts, some of us yearn for heroes with an edge—fangs and claws, whips and chains. Trouble is, we know we're not supposed to want those dark and dominant men. After all, we're equal to men now in all the ways that count. And that's just the way we want it.

Well, most of the time, anyway.

There's something seductive about the idea of making love to a man who may force us to explore our deepest, darkest impulses.

Now, the pitfalls of that need are obvious. How do we know that the handsome dom we pick up in a bar isn't a serial killer? How do we know that once he's got us tied up, he won't do something awful? Enacting those kinky fantasies is not easy to do in real life.

It's not even easy in fiction. I personally would be reluctant to write a heroine who deliberately sets about picking up a dominant in a bar, because doing so would make her Too Stupid to Live, for the same reason it would be a stupid thing for me to do in real life.

But we don't expect realism and logic from a fairy tale. In a fairy tale, you can believe in magic. You can even believe a woman might decide to stay with the Beast of her dreams or that a man might hack his way through a forest of thorns to find the beautiful woman of his fantasies. We don't worry about the logic of the character's actions, because fairy tales don't have to be logical.

And that makes these stories safe. The reader can relax and go along for the ride, enjoying the hot, luscious pleasure of the fantasy without worrying about the politics of a yen for submission or the intelligence of a heroine who would voluntarily stay with a Beast. After all, any story that begins with "Once Upon a Time" is not something to take seriously.

Then there are those six wonderful words: "And they lived happily ever after." You don't have to worry whether the heroine will be safe with her dominant prince, despite his taste for whips and chains. He will never hurt her—in a way she doesn't like, anyway. She's got her Happily Ever After. The story says so right there at the end.

So go pour yourself a glass of wine, light a few candles and settle down to enjoy. You may rest assured I will.

INTRODUCTION:
ONCE UPON
A TIME...

When I first put out a submissions call for erotic fairy tales, I did so with some apprehension. Ask anyone to name his or her favorite fairy tale and the answer is swift and decisive—these are the stories that stay with us our entire lives. So, I was nervous about what the response would be when I asked authors to take those beloved stories and spin them into erotic tales. I had fears that I would be answered only by the endless echo of my own voice in an abyss.

I needn't have worried.

The response to *Fairy Tale Lust* was overwhelming. Submissions started pouring in almost immediately, often accompanied by notes from the authors giving me background on their stories and reminiscing about their favorite traditional fairy tales. The submissions themselves were impressive in their variety. The reinterpreted versions of the classic fables had been lovingly crafted to remain true to the originals while giving them a new (and often kinky) twist. The tales that were new creations were written in voices that rang with an authenticity in the spirit of the classics. I was delighted with the stories that floated into my mailbox each week! And yet...a new apprehension grew in me. I felt like the princess presented with too many handsome beaus: how would I ever choose which ones to take? Would that every princess might suffer as I did!

The appeal of fairy tales is much like the appeal of erotica: both tap into our own deep desires and allow us to explore the boundaries of the taboo. When we are children, the whole world is foreign and new, and fairy tales give us a way to safely explore that world through imagination. As adults, often more jaded and cynical than we'd like to be, erotica lets us explore and redefine our ideas about sex and sexuality. We are given permission to want, to need and to try new things through the stories we read. Our imaginations are sparked by stories that surprise us with their ability to arouse. So many of those classic fairy tales are already layered with a subtext of sensuality. Beautiful women imprisoned; handsome men tortured; heroes and heroines undergoing tests of strength and will, seeking out the forbidden and exotic. It seems a marriage of lusty convenience to pair fairy tales and erotica. At last, those dusty old tales can come out of the closet and share their secrets!

The end result of my quest for erotic fairy tales is the book you hold in your hands. I owe a huge debt of gratitude to the wonderful Brenda Knight at Cleis Press for the many brainstorming phone calls and emails that led to the creation of this collection. Likewise, I cannot gush enough over the fabulous authors who took chances and pushed boundaries to write these one-of-a-kind stories. My only regret is that I couldn't have included more of the uniquely erotic tales I received.

From Delilah Devlin's traditional yet naughty "The Obedient Wife" to A. D. R. Forte's tale of a man discovering the depth of his submissive nature in "The Stone Room," and every story in between, *Fairy Tale Lust* has been compiled with the utmost love for the two genres it combines. The eroticism that was only hinted at in the original fairy tales is now laid out in naked splendor for your perverse pleasure. Take a walk in these dark woods and you're likely to come across all sorts of naughty mischief lurking in the gray shadows. Don't be afraid; the only pursuit here is one for your pleasure. Which story will be your favorite? Which one will speak to your darkest desire?

I invite you to turn the page and find out...

Kristina Wright
The dark woods of Virginia

THE OBEDIENT WIFE

Delilah Devlin

Once there was a miller who had no sons to work his mill or assure him comfort in his old age. His wife had died long ago giving him only a puny baby girl, whose worth didn't become apparent until she blossomed into a woman.

For then, her beauty stole the sunshine from the sky to sparkle in her fair hair. The birds grew mute when her lovely voice trilled. No truer blue or rosy hue could match the color of her eyes or soft, round cheeks.

To keep safe his only treasure, the miller locked her away inside their cottage while he considered how best to reap the rewards of his good fortune.

When it was time for her to wed, he sent a message to the village offering his precious daughter up for enough gold to see to his comforts for the rest of his life.

His announcement met with loud guffaws from the towns-people, for how could a scrawny, ugly man such as himself sire a creature worth the gold he demanded?

When no one offered him his fortune, the miller let one townsman inside his home to peer upon his bonny daughter. The man eyed her face, touched her soft golden hair, but he declared that her body must be misshapen and demanded to see more before he contemplated offering her bride price.

Now, the daughter was no fool. She knew her father meant to sell her to the highest bidder, but she'd spent her entire life inside her tiny house and longed to see more of the world beyond the confines of their small village.

So while she was willing to remove her gown and allow the townsman to look upon her naked flesh, she lashed out with a viperous tongue, letting him know she'd make the man who married her a miserable cuckold.

And yet more men came, offering her father gold, fine linens and furnishings to ogle her—enough gold to see to the peasant's comfort throughout his old age.

The daughter played upon her father's avarice, asking him why he should lower his sights to the townspeople when lords in neighboring demesnes would be willing to offer so much more.

The father set out to spread the word about his beauteous daughter, careful to avoid the subject of her temperament. While he was gone, the daughter continued to allow the men to visit, offering more to the married men among them than just the sight of her soft curves, for she knew the married men would keep their silence.

As she sank her mouth down the long slippery shaft of the barkeep, she counted in her head the coin she'd made, secure in the belief that only a few more days of service would provide her enough to buy her way to a port where she could sail to the edge of the world if she wanted.

"Aye, you've a talented mouth," the swineherd murmured, catching her hair at the back of her neck and forcing her to take him deeper in her mouth. "I'd pay more for the use of yer hot quim, girl."

She bit down, unmindful of his howls, and came off his long shaft. "Should that fool of a father of mine find me a rich husband, I will need to be a virgin."

The smithy, whose fat cock she stroked with her fist, patted her bottom. "There are other places a man can stick that a husband will never discover." He named a price that made her eyes light up with greed and she turned her bottom toward him, happily gobbling at the pig herder's cock while the smithy pushed his into her arse.

The moist sounds their bodies made and their agonized groans as they found their pleasure excited the girl, for the longer she withheld their pleasure, the more they were willing to pay for the release she offered. And though her jaws constantly ached, her hands felt as rheumy as an old woman's, and her ass was too sore for her to sit, she took her own pleasure in the tinkling of the gold that spilled into her secret stash.

While the daughter plotted her escape, her father traveled far and wide, seeking a suitor with deep pockets. When he approached a particularly wealthy village, he asked for the name of the richest among them. He was led to a castle deep in the wood, situated atop a small hill. The grounds were immaculate but deserted. He pounded on the door of the keep and trembled when it creaked open and a creature not quite a man nor all beast opened the door.

"Sir," the miller said timidly, "I seek the wealthy man who owns this keep."

"What business have you with him?"

"I've a treasure to offer him."

The beast stroked his hairy jaw. "What is the nature of this treasure?"

"The fairest woman in this land. A girl so beauteous even the roses bow to her when she passes."

"Is the girl obedient?"

The father cleared his throat. "She is as fair as the sun and moon."

"Does she obey?"

"She sings sweeter than a sparrow."

"Will she accept a husband's command?"

The father fought the quaver in his voice and said, "I have been told she is perfect in every way."

The creature eyed him and then smiled, revealing enormous teeth that made the old man's knees weaken.

"Bring her to me. If she is everything you promise, you will have your price."

The old man returned to his village, riding his old horse triumphantly through the streets.

"Miller, did you find a husband for that girl?" the smithy's wife shouted out.

"A finer man cannot be found."

The swineherd's wife passed him, giving him a narrow-eyed glare. "Will that girl of yers be leaving soon, old man?"

"She will, and she shall live like a princess in a castle."

"More fool's the lord who takes her," the woman muttered under her breath.

The miller paid the woman no mind, convinced she spoke from jealousy because of the perfection that was his daughter. When he returned home, he slammed open the door and called to his daughter.

A loud crash sounded inside the cottage, and she arrived at the door looking disheveled, her lips reddened and her skirts askew.

"Did I wake you, sweetling?" her father asked.

She glanced over her shoulder, then offered him a hesitant smile. "So, you're back. Did you find success in your journey?"

Her father grabbed her hands and nearly jumped, so great was his joy. "I've secured a fortune for you, girl."

She rolled her eyes and ushered him out of the house. "We must head to town to buy new gowns. How can I greet my husband in these rags?" She waved her hand behind her, confusing the old man.

"Is there a fly bothering you?"

She smiled and widened her eyes and waved her hand behind her again. A sound like a wild boar crashing through the brush behind the cottage drew his attention from her strange behavior.

"We needn't bother with shopping. Your husband will take you as you are. I've arranged a wagon, and this day we will begin our journey back."

And so it was that the miller's daughter traveled to the faraway village. The miller warned her as they approached the great keep's door. "Keep your words to yourself until he has paid."

The daughter smiled, nodding her assent, but she prepared a speech sure to wilt the lord's enthusiasm for this bargain. She had enough gold in her secret stash to see her way to the coast.

The door swung open and every word she'd rehearsed flew from her mind, because a great hairy beast dressed in trousers and boots and nothing more filled up the door. "This be the girl?" the beast rumbled.

The daughter shivered at the deep, warm sound, unsure whether it was pleasure or fear and also unsure which excited her more.

The miller smiled, pride lifting his chest. "This is the treasure I offer you."

"Come in. I would see whether the rest of her is as lovely as her face."

The daughter stepped quickly up the steps and began to draw her shift over her head. Standing naked beneath the creature's dark glare, for the first time in her life she felt a curling heat settle in her belly and moisture slide down her thighs.

The beast sniffed the air around her, trailed a claw along her shoulder. While he stood behind her, she could have sworn he licked her neck, and she trembled with the need for release from the sudden tightness of her quim.

The beast snorted and strode toward a chest from which he hefted a large bag of gold. He handed it to her father and ushered him to the door.

"B-but I would stay for the wedding!" her father stammered.

"Do you want the gold?" the beast asked, his voice deepening in warning.

Her father gulped and clutched the bag to his chest and left.

The beast turned slowly, stepping onto her shift, his long talons tearing at the fabric. "Is the air warm enough for you, my dear?"

Although she shivered, she nodded her head.

"Then you will have no need for this."

He walked away toward a long, stone staircase, and she scrambled after him, unwilling to be left in the drafty shadows below.

He paid her no heed as she wheezed, following him up and up to a tower room. Once inside, he set a large timber against the latch then turned to stare at her. "Are you afraid of me?"

"Should I be?" she asked, wondering if it was a trick question.

His eyes blinked, then a glower pulled his brows together and he approached her. "Are you not a virgin?"

She lifted her chin. "My woman's furrow has never been plowed, milord."

"And yet you do not blush."

"Shouldn't I be proud of my beauty? And since you will be my husband, 'tis your right to gaze upon my naked flesh."

He grunted and then lifted his chin toward the narrow bed in the center of the room. "I would have you rest now. I'll come to you in the darkness."

"But what about now? Don't you want…?"

A dark brow arched over his dark eyes, and she could have sworn a smile crimped one corner of his lips. "In darkness. Do not light a candle. I will be most unhappy if you do."

She nodded and then flopped down on the edge of the bed, her face falling with disappointment. "But I'm not tired."

The beast hesitated at the door. "Would you like…attention…before you sleep?"

Her eyes widened and color filled her cheeks. "Yes, milord… if it is your pleasure."

"The miller did not lie," he breathed. The beast strode toward her, coming to his knees in front of her. "Open your legs to me and fall back."

One long, wicked-looking claw gently traced the edges of her folds, and she wondered if she'd made a mistake. How could he see to her pleasure if he opened her flesh with a talon?

"I'll not harm you, sweetling."

She relaxed and closed her eyes, her breath catching at the first stroke of his tongue. Her quim clenched and he drew back. Then he lifted her thighs and placed them over his broad hairy shoulders, lifting her bottom from the mattress. When his mouth began to suckle her folds, liquid gushed to greet his tongue.

"I'm sorry."

He chuckled and kissed her between the legs. "You please me, beauty."

She settled with a satisfied sigh and dug her fingers into the edge of the mattress because the rasp of his tongue was a pleasure so great she wanted to shout, and she didn't want to spoil the moment with a shrill voice.

His tongue lapped around her entrance and stroked over the button at the top of her folds that she'd teased when the pig herder pumped inside her ass. But he licked away from it and she stifled her disappointment, only to gasp again when his unusually long tongue stroked inside her channel.

Unable to resist, she undulated her hips, sighing and gasping as he entered her over and over. When he stopped of a sudden, she moaned. "Why did you stop?"

"I fear the beast that I am will be overcome. You are so sweet, so responsive, and I mustn't take your quim until tonight."

"But there are other places a man…or beast…can take with his…member. Or so I've been told," she added breathlessly.

"You're too innocent for that kind of play, my dear."

"But I would please you, in whichever way you wish." She lifted her head to meet his dark gaze and offered him a smile.

He seemed to think about what she'd said, his eyes studying her, but she held her smile and kept her eyes open and innocent.

"Turn around and climb onto the edge of the mattress."

She did so, presenting her bottom to him eagerly.

He growled deep in his throat and more liquid dripped down one thigh. His tongue caught the trickle then smoothed up to clean her folds.

The miller's daughter moaned and widened her stance, dipping her back to offer him everything he wanted if he would just take her and be done with it.

His tongue trailed upward, past her folds to the tiny back entrance she found so deliciously sensitive. He swirled his tongue over it, parted her with his massive hands and thrust the tip of his tongue inside her.

The sensation was almost enough to send her to that place her clever hands delivered her nightly. He thrust and licked and thrust and licked until she forgot she wanted more.

But he withdrew, and the sound of clothing rustling stirred her excitement more. Something thick and firm prodded between her buttocks, and she found him bigger than even the smithy and breathed through her nose to calm her heart and ease the tightness of her arsehole.

He slipped inside, his breath catching, and she smiled with pride that she could please him. His great paws bracketed her hips, and he began to thrust against her bottom, tunneling deeper and deeper until she was sure he'd split her in two. Not that she minded. To die in the thrall of such immense pleasure was its own tortuous journey.

"Pleasure your nubbin," he growled.

"What, sir?"

"Use your finger to tease the knot at the top of your folds. I know you must know where it is and its purpose."

"I know it," she admitted. "'Tis how I kept myself virgin."

He reamed her ass, explosive thrusts slamming deep as she swirled her finger over the slippery knot, the tension in her belly building to a painful crescendo. "No more. I can take no more," she groaned.

"Then come for me, sweetling," he said, driving all the way inside her until the hair of his thighs abraded the insides of hers and his hairy balls clapped against her quim.

'Twas too much. Her back bowed and she howled long and loud, then collapsed to the bed, her naked breasts scraping on the fine counterpane beneath her.

His thrusts slowed; his growling became a steady, rhythmic purr.

When he stopped completely, she hid her face against the

mattress to hide how pleased and fulfilled she was.

He pulled free and turned her to her back, leaning his long hairy torso over hers, and gazed down at her with his frightening, black gaze.

She shivered, but realized it was not fear, not even a little bit. Her sex still convulsed in shallow pulses, and she wished she could know how it felt to accept his sex shafting deep inside her.

His gaze narrowed again, and he bent over her. His tongue lapped at her lips until she gasped and sucked it into her mouth. He pulled away and gazed down at her. "You are sure you are a virgin?"

"My quim has waited for one such as you, milord."

His face contorted into as near a smile as she imagined he could give. "Tonight. Close the curtains over the window. I will come to you again in darkness."

She rolled to the center of the bed when he made to leave and fell asleep within seconds.

That night, she stirred when the wind tossed the thick curtains cloaking the windows. She woke feeling drowsy, an ache in her arse and another more pleasurable one building between her legs.

The wooden door creaked open and a dark shadowy figure approached the bed. Her heart stilled for a second. "Milord?"

"'Tis I." His voice sounded softer, and she smiled in the darkness, having no doubts she'd pleased him earlier.

"You aren't frightened of me?"

"Of course not."

"I would ask for your obedience tonight. Unquestioned obedience."

Her body reacted to his request with surprising enthusiasm. She scissored her thighs to rub the moisture seeping from her body between them. "I will obey."

"You must raise your hands above your head and clasp the rungs of the headboard. You cannot let go, no matter what passes."

She liked this game more than she was willing to say and reached slowly above her head to wrap her hands tightly around the rungs.

"Now, open your legs wide and raise your knees. I want the cradle of your thighs completely exposed to me."

"Can you see me?"

"In all your splendor, my love."

She liked the way he said that, almost as though he meant it. So she parted her legs and raised her knees, letting them splay as wide as she could.

The mattress dipped at the foot of the bed and her heart began to beat wildly. "You will do it now?" she asked hoarsely. "You will take my virginity?"

"If that is what you offer me, then yes."

"It is yours, I swear."

"And yet your arse has known another man."

"I…" Her breath caught on a sob. "I have no excuse, can offer no apology. But I can tell you I took no carnal joy of the men who used my arse."

"Your pussy, it will be mine alone?"

"Yes."

"Then we will speak of the past no more. Do not touch me as I do this. You may not touch or see me. Promise me."

"I promise."

She felt the heat of him hovering over her, heard the sounds of him stroking his cock inside his palm, then felt the nudge of it against her quim. Her breath hitched and liquid spilled again.

"So sweet. So wet," he groaned, feeding his sex into her

channel, filling her with his thickness and thrusting only an inch or two inside.

"I want more. I can take more," she moaned.

"Slowly, I have no wish to harm you."

"I ache for you, milord. Fill me!"

He thrust forward, tearing past her virginity.

She howled then quaked beneath him, her body arching as pleasure and pain cut so deeply she feared she'd unravel like ribbon.

He thrust and bucked, but never so deeply she felt the fur around the base of his cock or the clap of his thick, hairy balls.

"Deeper," she cried out.

"'Tis as deep as I am meant to go. I'm nearly there." He thrust hard again, crowding through her slick walls, choking the throat of her womb—and it was enough.

Her body shuddered and jerked. She bit her lips to hold back her wild cries because she was hurtling fast toward the roof.

His shout echoed in the room, but he didn't linger after. He pulled away from her, climbing off the mattress and backing away from the bed.

"Why do you leave me?" she asked, sitting up, wondering if now that he'd had her maidenhead he no longer wanted her.

"I leave because I must. You will stay. You must keep away from me until morn. Promise me you will obey."

She promised, but as soon as she said the words, she wasn't sure she'd meant them.

He left her, his footsteps hurrying down the stone case.

The miller's daughter sat in the darkness, wondering what she'd done, how she might have displeased him. But another niggling worry entered her mind. All the while he'd taken her, she hadn't felt his coarse hair abrade her sensitive skin. Not anywhere. And his voice, while still a deep rumbling bass, didn't growl.

Had she even been swived by the same man?

She sat up and wiped the sheet between her legs to dry his seed and snuck out of the room, pressing her naked back against the cold stone wall as she slipped downward.

A light blazed in the hall he'd led her to when she first arrived. She took a deep breath and quickly peeked around the corner, but whoever was inside sat in a high-backed chair, facing a blazing fire.

She crept into the room as silently as she could, until the profile of the being sitting in the chair was clear. She gasped because he was the most handsome man she'd ever seen.

A dark, angry gaze swiveled her way, and a loud growl reverberated through the room. "You disobeyed me!"

The voice, although slightly thinner, was indeed her beast's, but she stared gape-mouthed at the creature in front of her—wholly male and as naked as she. Her body burned remembering how the shaft lying close to his brawny thigh had filled her. "It is you? Truly you?"

"Fool," he bit out. "It was all for naught."

"What, sir?" she said, reacting to the despair in his voice. "Tell me."

"You see this form that pleases you so? It was mine before I fucked a hag's daughter. When I refused to wed her because she was not virgin, her mother cursed me. Now I spend my days as the beast, my nights as a man. If I'd found an obedient wife, a virgin wife, I would have broken the curse. Now I'm damned to live out my life as neither fully man nor beast."

The miller's daughter's eyes filled with tears but she stepped closer despite the anger tightening his features. "This curse. What does it cost you?"

"I am a fearful sight. I frighten the villagers. They refuse to serve me. I fear they will one day revolt and murder me because

I am not human. And worse, I cannot touch a woman in passion for fear my talons might tear her flesh."

She licked her lips and crept closer still. "If another acts in your stead to acquire those services you miss, is not that problem solved?"

His eyes narrowed, but he gave her a swift, sharp nod.

"If another can acquire the staff and men-at-arms to properly see to your security, is not another problem solved?"

His chest rose and he nodded more softly this time.

"If you found yourself a wife willing to bed the beast and the man, would not the last problem be solved?"

His breath left in a long, pent-up sigh. "Yes."

She sniffed and tossed back her hair. "This nonsense about finding an obedient wife, you're not serious, are you?"

His beautiful smile took away her breath, and his hands shot out to grip her hips and bring her over his body to straddle his thighs. "I will demand obedience in only one place."

"And where will that be?" she whispered, a smile curving one corner of her mouth.

"The bedchamber, of course."

She leaned close to his mouth. "I will be a slave to your pleasure, milord."

He shifted her until his cock sought refuge in her silky, slick well. "Then I shall be your master, and happily so."

The miller's daughter smiled, for she had longed for adventure and to see amazing sights. Then pressing her hands upon his strong shoulders, she fucked the handsome lord until the shadow of the beast reawakened in his dark eyes.

HOW THE LITTLE MERMAID GOT HER TAIL BACK

Andrea Dale

O nce upon a time there was a woman who, after consuming enough vodka gimlets to loosen her tongue, finally dared to confess to her husband all the dark, delicious, dirty things she wanted done to her.

Unfortunately, her husband thought her desires were disgusting and degrading, and told her so in no uncertain terms. She stuffed those needs back into the dungeon of her subconscious and pretended it had all been a product of the gimlets; denied it was what she really wanted, who she really was.

Eventually, though, her husband left her for a perky and decidedly unkinky soccer-mom type, his parting words a sneer that his new wife wasn't some kind of perverted freak. Our heroine languished, alone and unfulfilled, seriously questioning whether what she wanted was normal and okay.

That really, really sucked.

Then she met Philip.

Philip wanted to hear about her fantasies. It was hard for

her to reveal them, though, after the betrayal, but he coaxed them out of her, bit by bit. He stroked her hair, held her close while she blushingly whispered her confessions. Then he fisted his hand in her hair at the base of her skull, held her immobile, and watched her as she gasped and trembled and tried to duck her head away, only to be jerked back by the pain.

"No, look at me. Tell me more."

Helpless, she did.

Our heroine (whom we'll call Ella) still couldn't tell him everything. There were things too kinky, too out there, too perverted, that she still feared would drive anyone away, even Philip. But as their relationship progressed, he showed an exceptional capacity for tapping into her secret desires, for anticipating what she feared and craved in equal measures.

She teetered on the knife edge of honesty and terror, and that's what made her come so hard, time after time.

It should be mentioned, because it's important to the tale, that Ella and Philip met professionally. He was an entrepreneur with a focus on restaurants, and she was a brilliant marketing strategist who knew just how to coax the public into descending in droves on any new venture she put her mark on.

After several successful restaurant openings and many, many intense sexual encounters that pushed her to her limits (or so she thought), they joined forces on Philip's newest venture, an upscale sushi joint.

"I was thinking about a big fish tank in the middle of the room," he said. "Exotic fish. Frilly, rare, eye-catching ones." Ella shivered as he smiled his wicked smile and added, "Deadly fish, even. Puffers, that sort of thing."

Mouth dry, she shook her head. Personal and professional warred. "Mermaid."

His eyebrows raised, as if she'd foolishly asked for mercy. "Mermaid?"

"A woman in a mermaid costume, in the tank," she said. In her mind, she could see it, like a burlesque swimming show, only updated and trendy and modern. Perfect for his type of restaurant. "Risqué, but not distasteful. Think Dita von Teese, but maybe not quite so distracting, because you'll want people focusing on the food. The food, though...it'll be daring, sexy."

"Audacious," he agreed, and the way he said the word sent thrilling tremors through her. "Encouraging people to take chances, face their hang-ups about food...and, subconsciously, other things."

She couldn't argue with him about that. He always took her ideas and tweaked them ever so slightly (or sometimes blatantly) to be about kink and deviance. And that worked, whether his patrons realized it or not.

Some of them did realize it, she knew with a delicious shudder. Some of them looked at her, consideringly, or even enviously.

They made a very good team.

She designed the ad campaign, started a buzz, made sushi sound like the most desired and deviant thing on the planet. She gave her input on the mermaid tank, and Philip listened intently and then rewarded her for her ideas.

There were always hiccups and panics as things got down to the wire, of course.

"We have a problem," Philip said. "We can't find anyone to be the mermaid." He cocked his head, watched her. Even without him touching her, she felt his gaze like a caress—if a caress could be defined as something that bored into her soul. "I think you should do it."

She sucked in her breath. His request sounded innocuous enough—she'd been a competitive swimmer in high school and college, was no stranger to pool or surf—but for her it held more. She wanted to please him. He made it sound like a light request, but in truth it was a command.

A command to which she acceded. Because Ella still didn't realize the depth of Philip's depravities.

Or, for that matter, how neatly they dovetailed with her own.

He didn't show her the mermaid outfit until that night, not until after she'd had her hair piled artfully atop her head and threaded through with strands of gleaming pearls, after her waterproof makeup was applied, after they were in the empty restaurant and she was admiring the tank in the center of the room.

The tank contained a soft faux "rock" shaped to perfectly cushion a lounging woman with her head and upper torso out of the water. Some filmy green plants were spaced to float in the water, which would be added once Ella settled herself in.

A wave generator would add some ripples, and fresh air would be pumped in to counteract the fact that a lid would enclose her.

Ella's sole job was to sit there and smile and occasionally run her hands through the treasure chest of gold coins and bright gems.

In Philip's office at the back of the restaurant, she stripped. She rather hoped he'd do something to her—spank her, maybe, to refresh the pain of the caning he'd given her a few days earlier. Her ass still bore the fading stripes, which felt a bit sore rather than outright stinging.

Instead he just watched her, his dark eyes glittering. She knew that look. It meant he had plans for her. Plans that would entail making her cry, making her come, making her soar.

He brought out the mermaid outfit.

First, the scallop shells that would cover her champagne-glass breasts. She'd assumed they'd be some sort of halter top, but oh, no. Just the shells themselves, with grooves on the insides that looked like they should hook to something. Her nipples weren't exactly the right shape...

That was when Philip produced the clamps.

Oh, sweet Poseidon.

Her breasts were sensitive, and once Philip had discovered that, he exploited the information at every given opportunity. Clamps, feathers, ice cubes, hot wax, and sometimes just sucking and tweaking until she came and couldn't stand being touched anymore and he didn't care and forced her to come again.

Ella loathed and craved breast play in equal measure.

That meant her nipples were already hard even before Philip tightened the clamps on them. She hissed against the pain as it transmuted to pleasure and back again.

"You will be beautiful tonight," Philip whispered in her ear. "You will be perfect. You will be mine."

Ella didn't have time to think about his words, because next he revealed her mermaid's tail.

She caught her breath. The scales shimmered and danced in emerald, sapphire and amethyst—not as bright jewel tones, but as muted undersea hues that flowed and sparkled like a prism.

When he helped her into it, she discovered how much more he had planned for her.

Thanks to the clamps and his very touch, she was already wet and open. She'd tried not to think about how aroused she was, about how she wished for his fingers or his cock or...well, if she'd wished for a dildo, she was certainly getting one now.

Built into the tail, the fake cock slipped into her, snugly filling her. She moaned and clamped down on it, and probably could have come right there if Philip's words hadn't penetrated her haze.

"Not yet, my sweet."

Not yet, but how long, how excruciatingly long would he make her wait?

The tail pressed her legs together, fitting firmly but comfortably around her waist. She couldn't touch herself, couldn't move her legs, couldn't thrust against the dildo.

If she concentrated, she could probably clench down rhythmically and bring herself off. Probably? Definitely, given her aroused state. But he'd told her not yet, and she'd already agreed that he was in charge of when she came. The problem was that the dildo, hard and pressed into her and undeniably *there*, would keep her stimulated the entire time.

She took a deep breath. She could get through this.

She repeated that to herself when Philip snicked the tail closed with a tiny lock. He'd release her when he was good and ready; she had no control.

Once the shells were hooked to the clamps—sending a fresh wave of pleasure through her—Philip rolled her out to the restaurant floor on a cart, and he and a waiter positioned her in the tank.

As the comfortably warm water rose, he kissed her forehead. "Do you trust me?"

She found the question strange. "Of course I do."

He covered the tank. She was left with the faint humming sound of the motor and the swishing ripples of the water. She languidly flipped her tail up and down, amused by the sensation and the waves she created. Of course, the motion also made the dildo rock inside her. She smiled. She'd enjoy this tease because later, their sex would be incredible.

The first guests arrived, peering into the tank before accepting champagne and mingling. She waved at them.

Then she caught her breath as her entire groin vibrated to

life. Eyes wide, she sought out Philip in the crowd. Saw him smiling. Saw him palming the remote control that operated the clit vibe and made the dildo squirm inside her.

Was he serious? Did he really think she could keep from coming if he manipulated her like that?

Then she heard his voice and realized there was a speaker in the tank.

"Sweet mermaid, I would never torture you by denying you pleasure tonight. You have my permission to come at will, as often as you wish."

Was he serious? Did he really think she could come here, now, surrounded by people and on display?

Did she really think she couldn't?

The vibrations weren't up to the max; in fact, he toyed with the remote, sometimes turning it up high, sometimes turning it off completely. Even as he chatted with guests, he watched her.

She was drenched, inside and out. Whenever she shifted, she felt her juices pooled and slippery inside the tail. Nobody else could tell; nobody else knew how aroused she was, what sweet torture she suffered.

Then, when the room was full, and the guests nibbled sushi, Philip cranked up the remote control and nodded at her.

No. Her mouth formed the word, a pursed O, but she didn't make a sound. It wouldn't have mattered anyway, because he couldn't hear her; the only thing that would make him stop was if she pushed the button near her right hand, which would release the top of the tank in case of emergency.

She didn't want to come in front of a roomful of people, but the choice wasn't hers, never had been hers. She was Philip's; she'd given herself to him. She hadn't lied when she'd said she trusted him.

The sensations were too much. The buzzing against her clit

and the writhing dildo inside her built the pressure to dizzying heights. She barely had time to press her hands against the sides of the tank before the orgasm slammed through her.

She thrashed as she came, her tail slapping against the water, her back arching, her shell-clad breasts thrusting up and out.

She opened her eyes and tried to compose herself as her climax subsided to gentle pulses. She managed a weak smile at the guests who stared at the tank and flipped her tail as if to say, "Just part of the act."

But Philip didn't turn down the remote, and she felt another orgasm building inexorably, and again she was helpless to stop it.

He made her come again and again, delighting (she was sure) at her wriggling and squirming and thrashing, her struggles to pretend she wasn't coming her brains out in front of a roomful of people.

"Everything okay, my sweet?" he asked during a reprieve.

Cheeks flaming, she nodded.

And he turned the remote to the max again.

Somewhere in the middle of an orgasm, or perhaps in one of the mindless moments between, Ella felt something inside her crack open. The words her husband had left her with—*dirty, disgusting, perverted*—had hardened and lodged deep in her psyche, blocking her acceptance of who she was, what she wanted. Philip had chipped away at her shame, but now fractures fissured through it.

Opening her eyes, she again sought Philip out in the crowd. As their eyes met, he asked again, "Do you trust me?"

She nodded.

And then felt a fresh wave of fear and humiliation and arousal crash over her as she watched him hand the remote control to the woman standing beside him.

The original story of "The Little Mermaid," she remembered,

was that the mermaid had given up her tail for the love of a man, and he'd betrayed her and left her in constant pain.

Now, she understood. She trusted Philip to the point that he could share her with others. She was his prized, beloved possession, and he wouldn't share her unless it was with reverence and respect.

He'd given her back her belief that she wasn't wrong, or different, or broken.

He'd given her back her tail.

Another climax built, and Ella welcomed its freedom.

You can bet they lived happily ever after.

DUCKING

Craig Sorensen

H ave you heard the one about the ugly duckling? As a girl my ears were too big, my nose was too big, my eyes were too wide set. My lips were thin and my cheekbones too sharp. I was long and gangly with strong, exaggerated limbs and large joints.

Kids can be cruel, and no one knows this wrath more than the ugly duckling. So she hangs on to the whole swan thing. By the age of twenty, not much had changed, but I was taller with bigger breasts and fuller hips. I learned to blend in, no mean feat when you stand six foot one. But I did master the art of the uncomely Ninja:

Ninja vanish.

Ninja disappear.

Ninja duck.

Only in my work did I stand out. By then, my intelligence and drive became an asset. At least I had a beautiful brain; I lavished all I could upon it.

I married young, a man who could appreciate me for what I was: neurotic, driven, intelligent, skilled at mechanics and yard maintenance, able to make money hand over fist.

Jason said over and over how he loved my "rare sense of humor." He finally tested that sense of humor when, after twenty years of marriage, a younger woman took a fancy to him. See, he hadn't been all that much to look at either, but when he got his weight under control, offset by a nice fat bank account...

Well, yes, I laughed.

Ninja laugh.

Walking down a long, nearly empty hall of the mall, I pulled my long hair back from my face and a cute teenaged boy nudged his friend, pinky extended in my direction. "Check out the MILF."

I turned and they looked away, subverting grins and angling their eyes alternately toward me as they lowered their voices to whispers punctuated by giggles.

I wasn't sure I wanted to know what sort of "ugly" thing a MILF was. I gave in and Googled it.

An older, sexually attractive woman.

Mothers I'd Love to Fuck.

I clicked on the "images" link, and this assortment of sexy, mature women filled the screen.

First, I wasn't a mother. One of the kindest things Jason and I ever did for anyone was the deference we made for our unborn children. We left them unborn. As little sex as we had, this was not such a challenge.

But the *I'd Love to Fuck* part was what left me stunned. I tried to recall if there might have been another woman near me. That had to be it, otherwise these boys, so far from the mental institution they had escaped, needed to be promptly re-incarcerated. Or maybe the drying ink on my divorce papers and the lack of sex, no matter how sparse, made me interesting: an old doe, especially ripe in desperate estrus before two lonely, delusional young bucks.

Then I realized what I should have known all along. I'd seen it enough in my day: sarcasm.

I pulled the old mower out of the shed and started my usual ritual of fighting to get it to start. It was being extrastubborn and I was thinking I just might finally give up and buy a new one. I continued to pull the cord. *Crackita! Crackita! Crackita!* I'm nothing if not determined.

"Hi, I'm Evan." I jumped like a startled rabbit. His dark skin glowed above tight, white bicycle shorts. "Sorry! Can I be of some assistance?" He was a young neighbor who had passed me a hundred times since moving in to the townhouse a few doors down. He'd always politely nodded and greeted me.

I knew this old mower inside and out. I had already calculated what the problem was. "Thanks, I've got it covered."

A trim goatee framed his smile, black stubble lit up his sparkling dark brown eyes. "You sure?"

"Yeah, I'm good."

He tilted his head and gave a strange smile: friendly, but wistful. "Well, okay, but if you ever, you know, need anything." He turned back to his townhouse, his young, strong butt perfectly cradled in the tight shorts. I opened my mouth but had no words.

He pulled a bicycle from his garage in the back and started down the alley away from me.

I watched him disappear and got my mower started.

I pulled down my loose sweatpants and took off an oversized white T-shirt with the logo of a prospective vendor at work on it, then my utilitarian panties and started for the shower. I paused at my computer where the results of my "MILF" query remained behind the screen saver. I shook the mouse and looked at the women who had come up in my unfiltered image search. In the bathroom my sweaty skin, long body and large features reflected in the one mirror in the house confirmed they were not in stride with these gorgeous women.

But I did see my face differently. Whatever looks I had at twenty, I pretty much had at forty-two; I hadn't changed much.

It was the standard joke: my amazing sense of smell was because of my large nose. It picks up the slightest scents at amazing distances. My ex even doubted I could smell some of the things I said I could.

But there was no doubt that I could smell him every time Evan came out of his place two doors down. His odd sunscreen eventually brought out a Pavlovian response: my vagina got wet and my nipples pointed like oversized pencil erasers. I even took to wearing bras when I mowed, never really a requirement as my tits were gravity proof, but useful now as camouflage.

Ninja suppress.

I seized every opportunity to be in the backyard that summer. Watching Evan in my extraordinary peripheral vision became my favorite spectator sport. He usually wore those tight shorts, flip-flops and nothing else. As I dug for new plants, added fresh mulch, or just watered, I eyed him.

He always waved and gave that smile. I tried not to duck when he caught my eye. I drew on him when I covered up tight in my king-sized bed, spread my long legs and worked my clit to orgasm. Funny, but the bulge in his shorts was only an accent spice. It was that look that drove me on. I continued to catalog every expression, all the while ducking.

* * *

I stood before the long mirror and examined the new suit that I had tried on for size, a long, broad skirt beneath an oversized jacket. It was in step with what I always wore.

"That's not such a good fit for you."

I jumped. The young salesgirl had managed to approach with the stealth of a KGB operative. She was pretty and smelled like a garden. "Sorry if I surprised you."

I shrugged. "S'okay."

"What I meant was, if your thighs are half as nice as your calves, you should wear something shorter. And they hang too loose."

"I like them that way."

"For comfort?"

"Um, yeah. I guess."

The salesgirl tilted her head. "You know you've got ripping calves, right?"

"Oh, come on, they're kind of thick—"

"Kind of? They're great! The athletic look is so in, and you're so at the top end of the scale. I mean, you must work out all the time, right?" She chomped her gum and pulled her glasses from her face and looked at my camouflaged hips as if through a magnifying glass.

"A bit." I'd bought one of those machines with the big springs I'd seen during a bout of insomnia in the death throes of the divorce proceedings. It filled some time.

"I know women who put in hours a day and don't look like you. You need to get a look that fits you. I mean, no offense—"

"Um...none taken." I looked at myself in the mirror.

"Humor me. Will you take off your jacket?" The pretty salesgirl pinched the top of my lapel and gently shook it for emphasis. I removed it and she sighed. "Jeez, the blouse looks like a tent."

I looked down and shrugged. "I like them like this." I hadn't felt this defensive since grade school.

"Then why do you look so awkward?" She reached toward my waist. I could feel the heat of her fingers. "May I?"

"Well...okay."

She touched my blouse and waited. I finally nodded cautiously. "Go ahead. I'd—I'd like to know...what you think." I wasn't sure that I did want to know.

She patted my waist like a male cop doing a pat-down of a female suspect. She smoothed my hips. "Damn, you got great hips. I mean..." She licked her fingertip and pressed it to the upper part of my butt and made a *ssss* sound. "Hot, girl."

I laughed out loud. "You have a wicked sense of humor, um..." I studied her name tag. "Monica."

She continued to eye my upper body. She pulled my blouse tight at the waist, so it squeezed at my breasts. "Do you wear a bra?"

I slowly shook my head.

She whistled and I looked around to see if she'd attracted any attention. She acted like she was going to feel me up. My pussy drained into my panties. It occurred to me that maybe my hard looks were that way for a deeper reason. Maybe I was a latent lesbian.

"You really shouldn't dress like this. You can't hide your assets." She winked.

"My body isn't great, by any means. I mean, big joints and muscles, I'm gangly..." I was ready to continue the whole litany of shortcomings.

"Shit, are you serious? You don't know how 'in' your look is? Masculine is the new feminine."

I blurted a laugh.

"I'm not kidding. You don't know that?"

"Nonsense."

"Whatever." She swept one hand dismissively. She turned to leave.

"What did you have in mind, Monica?" I called after her.

She took my hand in hers. "Come on!"

She brought me bright suits and dark blouses, then dark suits and bright blouses. The skirts were universally short, well up my long hard thighs.

I was almost dizzy from trying things on. She approved some of her choices, dismissed others. I showed her each outfit. "Work it, girl!" I tried to do little model-style swirls. "Gawd, you got great knees!"

I was now certain this girl was just stroking me. Around $5,500 worth of clothes hung on a rack to one side. I couldn't imagine I'd ever wear them.

"So, should I wrap 'em up? They look great on you."

My duck reflex was strong, but my pussy was dripping and my heart hadn't throbbed so hard at my last two-hour workout. My sigh was a delicious surrender. It was not like I didn't have the money. "Wrap 'em up." Maybe just having them in my closet would somehow be like the *Playgirl*s I stashed between the mattress and box spring when I was a teenager.

Monica again reached for me, this time my face. She waited for me to nod. She pulled my long hair tight behind my skull. "At least put your hair in a ponytail so you can show off your face. Better still, cut it short. Oh, and about your makeup..." She held out a business card.

"My makeup? What about it?" My mother had taught me to put on makeup. I'd always done it this way, never really thought about it. No way I'd go to someone for makeup. I shrugged and she started to retrieve the card.

It occurred to me that I looked more like my dad. I reached out like a greedy child and Monica gave me the card.

* * *

I bought new, revealing workout wear using some of the ideas that Monica had given me. These I wore regularly—with the shades closed, of course—then worked in the yard in my loosest sweats, hair dangling like a nice curtain.

One morning the scent of Evan's sunscreen filled the kitchen. The wetness between my legs grew as I thought of his smile and the looks and encouragement of the salesgirl. I knew I wasn't a lesbian; it was that the young woman treated me as attractive. I still believed that she was just stroking me, making what turned out to be an extravagant sale...

Of clothes that hung like still lifes in the walk-in closet.

The richness of Evan's scent overtook the kitchen and my heart pounded harder.

Before I could duck, I changed into a pair of tight sweat-shorts that barely covered my hips and a spaghetti strap top that exposed a strip of my muscular waist. I returned downstairs and held the doorknob in my hand. I rushed back up and applied the new makeup as I had been recently taught; I'd expected her to show me how to make my eyes more closely set, my nose smaller, my lips fuller. Far from it; she showed me how to adorn what I was. I looked weird in the mirror.

Probably the hardest thing of all was to tie my long hair to the top of my head.

I rushed downstairs and pulled in a breath like I was about to dive in frigid water. I even locked my door behind me as I exited it to impede my easy return inside.

I felt scared; I felt freed. I wanted to duck with the conviction of an ostrich. I probably looked like a frightened rabbit hearing the screech of a falcon diving. After a few deep breaths, I walked with a gait like it was no big deal, though I'm sure my pencil-top nipples on this ninety-five degree day belied my pretenses. I didn't look at Evan but regretted my wicked peripheral vision, which saw him clearly.

He stood in the middle of his perfectly manicured lawn, head turning like a turret. I was more a spectacle than I had thought. I didn't dare look Evan's way; I just opened the combination lock to my shed and stepped inside the oven-hot room and lingered. Perhaps I could just hide there. It was so miserably hot. I pulled the mower out, thinking it might make a good cover.

Evan stood poised over his mower, too, until I looked. He pulled the starter on his brand-new mower deliberately, eyes darting between it and me. *Crackita. Crackita, crackita!* He shrugged like a helpless woman with a flat tire on the freeway.

My stomach did loop-de-loops. My pussy was draining so hard that my only solace was that the shorts I'd chosen were black.

He called out. "You know anything about these things?"

I nodded. He wiped his brow in exaggerated relief. I joined him and looked down at the front of the mower. The spark plug was disconnected. His eyes slowly measured me. I lifted the cord and his eyebrows rose high. "You look great, Lisa," he whispered. "You always look good, but right now..." The bulge in the front of his shorts grew huge, the shape of his rod became clear. He casually folded one large hand in front of it. "Um...sorry."

Right up to that very second, I'd harbored doubts that this was all just a cruel game. I'd stood ready to duck yet again. I sighed. "Sorry?" I peeked around his guarding hand.

"Can I offer you an iced tea...um, inside, Lisa?"

I drew a fresh, deep breath. "Please." I followed him with a slow, cautious gait.

* * *

When I reached for my hair tie to release my curtain, Evan gently grabbed my wrist. "I'd like it if you left it up."

"Well...okay."

We stood at the big stainless steel fridge looking at it. "I can't stand it anymore." He grabbed me and pressed my back to it. "The tea will keep."

I laughed nervously until he pressed a deep kiss into my mouth.

Though Evan was a bit taller than me and his muscles well defined, I would not have believed he could lift a woman my size with such ease. He gripped gently under my pits and lifted me until my head draped over the top of the appliance. I stared at the ceiling and focused as he nibbled up and down me, popped my top over my tits with his teeth, then my shorts down to my knees. I felt paralyzed.

It was appropriate that we were in the kitchen. He nibbled my ribs, licked my belly button, flicked my hard nipples and sucked them until I felt exquisite pain. He moaned and made snarling noises as he ate more and more of me. He squeezed me to his chest, my pussy pressed to the ridge at the front of his silky shorts. I curled my long legs around his back, gripped tightly to his thick neck. "Please don't let me go, Evan."

"Are you kidding?" His kisses were salty and savory as he probed my mouth. I'd never felt like this before: a possession, the object of desire, needed as much as wanted. He fought the top of his shorts down, and his subdued cock sprang out like a demented jack-in-the-box and slapped between my buttcheeks. We shared a laugh that continued right up until his cock plunged deep in me.

He carted me around his townhouse, seemingly suspended on his cock. He set me on the dining table, pumped me hard, then plopped me on his couch and fucked me even harder. He lifted me high and shoved me to a tall table in the entryway, knocking a vase over and sending two Lautrec prints askew. The dried flowers scattered on the travertine floor.

He didn't miss a stroke, even as the vase bounced like a basketball. It rang like a bell and miraculously didn't break.

It was as if he was marking his territory with…well, with me. Eleven rooms total, until he placed me like a gemstone in a velvet-lined box, on the surface of his bed in the master suite. I reached to pull a corner of the silk bedspread back.

"Don't you dare cover even an inch."

He pulled my shorts from my ankle and eased my top over my head. For the second time, he devoured me.

All the years I had gone down on my ex to reward him after an uninspired lick or two between my legs seemed to come back to full payment as Evan worked my folds, my hips lifted to his mouth, my curled legs bobbing in time with his ravenous eating. I went rigid as he goosed that first orgasm from me. I'd never felt anything like it, not even from my most inspired masturbation. I yelled out over and over, and this only seemed to urge him deeper. The orgasm lingered on, my belly strained like infinite ab crunches.

He let my hips avalanche. I lay sprawled, body heaving, limbs still as fallen branches. I panted.

He smiled gently and traced my face slowly with thick fingers. "May I make love to you, Lisa?"

After all this, after all he had taken, after all he had given, his asking this now drew from deep inside me. Tears, pent up over ducking ten thousand times, exploded from me.

"Oh, god, did I hurt you?" He held a Kleenex box toward me.

I cried even harder into tissue after tissue. Between sobs I managed syncopated sentence fragments. "Didn't hurt. Far from. Please. Make love. Please, Evan."

He rushed to his dresser and feverishly dug in drawer after drawer until he produced a new box of condoms that he ripped open like a Christmas present. The strip of condoms dangled like a Chinese ribbon dance as he raced back to the bed. While I composed from my tears, he squeezed a rubber on, then stroked my face and eased back inside me.

His hips curled so very slowly. He seemed not to want to orgasm as he lingered on his thick arms, every detail of his sheathed rod tactile in me. He alternated hands and stroked my clit methodically, until he led me to another orgasm. His mouth finally gaped like a gator's and he held his breath. His eyes went wide and fixed on mine as he grunted over and over.

A small drop of drool fell like the first raindrop at the end of a drought and glazed my left nipple.

He collapsed hard to my chest and kissed along my shoulders and neck and face as his cock softened in me.

My waist clenched in what I can only describe as my first spontaneous orgasm.

I donated every last bit of my frumpy clothes. My old makeup went out with some bread that had gone moldy. The bright new clothes in my closet were like new flowers planted where the weeds had just been pulled, and for once I was clipping them to show them off.

My head felt so light after that first draconian haircut.

"Lisa!" I didn't jump, didn't tug the short hem of my new skirt down, but I almost ducked as a coworker stood at the entry to the break room. His eyes traveled down my new, bright feathers. "You look great!"

"Thanks, Mark." I'm still having a hard time believing that

I've grown into a swan so late in life, but I'm starting to believe that I'm not half bad for a duck. After an uneasy moment, I drew a refreshing breath and walked with a relaxed gait from the break room and his eyes followed.

Ninja strut.

THREE TIMES

Justine Elyot

And so it was that a Proclamation went out across the land, from the river basin to the mountain villages, that whosoe'er should free the Princess from the shackles of vine would win her hand.

That day was a busy one in the Market Tavern, and Selina was rushed off her feet, running from barrel to bar top to table and back, trays of foaming beers held aloft in both hands so that all she could use to bat away the constant barracking and groping was her sharp tongue. Between bouts of flirtation, the likely lads of the town formulated foolproof plots to unbind the Princess from her obstinate tethers and claim her for their own.

"She is fair—she will look well in my bed." General guffawing assailed Selina's ears, and she uttered a silent prayer that the unlucky Princess might find a more gallant rescuer than these thickset, foul-mouthed baboons.

"Can you imagine it—to make your fortune and to fuck it too!"

"To fortune and fucking!" The toast was proposed and the

tankards clinked together, spilling foam into Selina's cleavage as she passed. *Fortune and fucking*, she thought. The prospect of either was as remote as the Utopian Peninsula. She went to the back room to fetch the mop.

Princess Ellora had never looked so serene, so beautiful or so heartbreaking. Against the bark of the silver vine tree she stood, still as a statue, her arms arched gracefully above her head. Some of the tree's pearlescent sheen had transferred to her skin, giving her an unearthly glow on those parts of her body that were unveiled; to the rest, a togalike silken garment clung, outlining the teardrop shapes of her breasts and her lean, young hips. She looked like an exotic dancer, caught and frozen in midslink, her lips parted and the dark almonds of her eyes held in an expression of melting desire. But for whom was the Princess feeling this eternal moment of exquisite lust? Her arms and legs were crisscrossed with winding vines and, although her dress protected some vestiges of her modesty, it was clear that the snakelike plants holding her in bondage were also performing a secondary task.

The King sighed as he pulled aside the gauzy material to apprise his Lord Chancellor of the full seriousness of his daughter's plight.

"Good heavens!" exclaimed the veteran politico. "Good… merciful…heavens."

And he had to retrieve his lorgnettes to make sure that he was seeing straight, for the vines slithered all the way up Ellora's thighs, cutting into their white succulence, and then they passed between her labia to disappear inside her. Around her breasts they were also tied, then wound around her nipples before curving back past her hips. Pressed against the vine's eerily phosphorescent bark, Ellora's buttocks were not visible, but it seemed fair to assume that the invasive plant was making its presence felt there as well.

"Does she...feel anything?" whispered the Lord Chancellor.

"I cannot tell. Her heart beats, and the blood still flows in her veins...but she has neither moved nor spoken since the vine claimed her."

"What is this vine? I have seen nothing similar before."

The King extended his hands, wringing them in frustration. "I do not know! Nobody knows! I have had all the botanists in the land examine it, but they cannot pinpoint its provenance. We know that it is unbreakable and poisonous to the touch. Ellora stumbled into the leaves and was instantly bound tight. We have tried knives, saws, even blowtorches—nothing seems to affect it."

"And now you fall back on general competition? With the offer of Ellora's hand as bait? Dear me, Your Majesty, there are laws governing a lady's right to choose her own match now, you know. Could I advise a different reward? Some lands? A diadem or two?"

"A diadem or two won't cut it," snapped the King. "And besides, once some backwoods oaf has used his unexpectedly magical axe to free my Princess, we can always...renegotiate..."

"Renegotiate, Your Majesty?"

"Fling him in gaol on a charge of assault or attempted murder or something." The King shrugged. "Obviously I have no intention of tainting our bloodline."

"Ah. I see."

"Well, then. Let us waste no more time. Open the gates and admit the pretenders."

Selina saw them all, a steady stream of dejected faces trooping into the Market Tavern and calling for ale, one after another after another.

"No luck?" she would ask sympathetically, and he would

slam down his pocketknife or diamond cutter or shovel on the table and launch into his tale of failure.

Summer turned to autumn, and the vine held fast, showing no signs of shedding leaves or shriveling naturally, as had been the King's faint hope. Ellora's pulse continued to jump at her wrist, and experts thought that perhaps the vine was nourishing her in some way, for she appeared in perfect health, her cheeks rosy and hair glossy as ever.

One dark afternoon in late November, a visitor from out of town appeared at Selina's bar. These had been many and frequent during the summer, at the height of the competition, but were trailing off now, so the man's unfamiliar visage and mode of dress caught Selina's eye. It was no more than his foreignness that piqued her curiosity, for he was a fusty old fellow, bony-fingered and with a high dome of a forehead over a beaky nose. He drew his cloak tightly about him, seeming to find the air in the town unexpectedly frigid.

"Are you from a warm place, sir?" asked Selina politely, setting down a pint of ale and a trencher of bread and cheese.

"Yes," he said. "Doesn't the rawness make your bones ache?"

"Oh, we are used to it, sir. We have just had a beautiful summer, so it doesn't seem so bad."

He smiled at this, an odd, unsettling smile. "Yes," he said. "All the same, I'll trouble you for a brandy, if I may. This chill does not agree with me."

"What brings you to our land?" asked Selina, setting a tot of the amber warmer in front of her guest.

"Curiosity," he smiled over the rim of the glass. Then a frown chased the remnants of merriment away. "And revenge."

"Revenge?"

"I cannot tell you. It must remain in my thoughts until my plan has succeeded."

Now, if Selina had one fault—and, although generally an excellent girl, she was not quite faultless—it was an inability to resist the lure of a good story. And here, right in front of her, was what promised to be one of the best tales she might ever hear. So she closed the tavern and plied her guest with more brandy, until both his inhibitions and his tongue were loosened.

"Oh, yes," slurred the visitor, twisting locks of Selina's hair in his bony fingers and breathing brandy-soured breath into her face, "your King will rue the day he tangled with August Villiers."

"But are you sure you will be able to kill the vine and claim the hand of the Princess?"

"Quite, quite sure, you naughty wench." He attempted to slide an arm around Selina's waist, but she shifted sideways, away from the creeping tendril of his limb. "Why are you blowing hot and cold?" he lamented. "Come to bed and I'll split the fortune with you."

"Later. Tell me how you will do it. No man has succeeded—it is said to be impossible to kill."

"Well, it is. Unless you are the man who planted it, and you know its secret."

"You are the man who planted it?"

"I am. I am the owner of Villiers Vines; I specialize in the hybridization and cultivation of rare vines. This one has a curse on it."

"Cursed by you?"

"No, by a powerful and malign wizard of my acquaintance. In his youth, your King did me a great wrong. I have plotted my vengeance ever since...and now it is complete."

"What did he do?"

"He stole my sweetheart from me."

"Ah. He does have that reputation."

"Rightly so. When his daughter was born, I sent the vine

as an anonymous gift. He planted it, little knowing that it was cursed to imprison the child as soon as she reached the age of one and twenty."

"Marriageable age?"

"Indeed."

"But the Princess has not wronged you. She is innocent in all of this."

Villiers shrugged. "Collateral damage."

Selina narrowed her eyes. "So how will you free her?"

The visitor chuckled dryly. "The vine will release the Princess and die once she has...come. Three times."

"Come?" Selina shook her head. "Come where? I don't understand."

"You don't understand what it means to come? I'd love to show you," leered Villiers.

"Oh! I see!" Selina's hands flew to her cheeks, which were stained scarlet. "I understand! Goodness!"

Villiers held out a hand. "And now I must invite you to... come with me." He guffawed at his own dirty joke.

"Just one more brandy—to keep our blood on fire," suggested Selina, hopping behind the bar and pouring a double measure, into which she tipped a few drops of a sleeping draught she kept there for emergency use. It came in very handy when the tavern was packed with rival Dragon Racing teams—one dose and the warring factions fell into peaceful slumber.

Once Villiers lay snoring, cheek flattened to the trestle table, Selina lit a lamp and hastened out into the night.

Up the winding cobbles she toiled, toward the castle that perched at their summit, looming over the town like a magnificent bird of prey.

Her friend Elrond was on guard tonight, as she had hoped, and she flitted up behind him, pinching his bottom so that he jumped and nearly dropped his halberd.

"Who goes there?" he yelped, but Selina's giggles gave him his answer; in a trice he had spun around and caught her about the waist, drawing her against his armored chest. "Somebody wants a spanking," he growled.

"Mmm," she agreed in a low purr. "If you keep your gloves on."

"I'm off duty at six," he told her. "I'm not having you in the sentry box again—if we'd been caught, I'd be in the dungeons now."

"Spoilsport," Selina pouted. "It was exciting, though, wasn't it?"

He smiled and kissed her in reply. "So," he said, drawing back with a final nip to her lips. "What are you up to?"

"Must I be up to something?"

"Knowing you, yes. Why are you here?"

"Elrond, I can't stop thinking about the Princess, all tethered and tied by those creepy vines. I long to see her."

"It's quite a sight."

"Have you seen...under her clothes?"

"No. Only the King and Queen are permitted."

"Wouldn't you like to see? I've heard tell that the vines enter her body, through her sex. It must be quite an...arresting picture."

"We'll get arrested, you mean, if we're caught looking."

"Elrond, it's very late. Everybody is asleep. Who can catch us looking? That's your job."

"Selina..."

"The idea of seeing her, tied and penetrated by that plant, is unbearably arousing to me, Elrond. Please, just let me see. Please."

Elrond had been tempted many times when patrolling that area of the garden, but so far, fear had kept him from succumbing.

However, the thought of Selina growing wet and wanton at the sight of the Princess's beautiful bound body proved too much for him.

"Well...all right. But we mustn't stay for long. A quick peek and then we come straight back. And I'll have to spend the rest of this sentry duty with an almighty erection, I suppose."

"I'll make it worth your while."

"You certainly will," he said grimly, taking his bunch of keys and unlocking the castle gates.

Once inside, Selina set off at a barefoot run through the castle grounds while Elrond, having to be stealthy in his clinking armor, struggled to keep pace with her.

By the time she had reached the arbor where Princess Ellora languished in her tentacular prison, Elrond was far, far behind. From the arch that led into the garden, Selina could see the silver shimmer of the vine's bark, calling her toward it. She gasped as, step by step, the Princess's plight was revealed in full and frightening clarity.

Now that she was close to the captive girl, she began to doubt Villiers's tale—how could somebody so seemingly unconscious be brought to the sweetness of climax?

Nonetheless, she was resolute, and her step did not falter until she was close enough to smell the faint perfume of the Princess's skin, mingled with the sharp vegetable tang of the vine. Selina's instincts told her that she should not touch the treacherous bonds but limit her contact to the human flesh on display. She drew aside the flimsy garments and dropped to her knees, inspecting the tangle of plant and pleasure spot, assessing how best to go about her unusual task.

Although the root passed through Ellora's lower lips, it had wound itself around her clitoris so that the shiny pink button stood out proudly. The silvery skein was easy to avoid. Selina put out a hand, slowly, almost afraid that the vine would rear up and lash her away, but it did not. Instead, her forefinger touched the Princess's clit, jiggling it a little to ascertain how tender it was. It felt a little dry to the touch, but once Selina had stroked it for a minute or so, it grew slick and easier to manipulate. Selina fell into a diligent rubbing motion, sometimes stroking with finger and thumb, sometimes pressing her palm against the tiny morsel, watching it grow and swell beneath her touch. For all the obvious evidence of arousal, the Princess's body remained impassive, held tight by its silver-green chains, but Selina noticed that, as the clitoris fattened, the vines began to swell inside her sex, and then to begin a gentle thrusting.

The first coming was sudden and over almost before it began; the smallest swivel of her hips led to a parting of her lips and a brief burst of exhalation. But the vines slackened noticeably, and Selina gasped, astonished at the power she had over this poor creature.

Concerned that she might chafe the sensitive bud if she worked it too hard, she decided to use her tongue for the next stage. She had never tasted a clitoris before, but this one was warm and sweet and luscious, certainly a lovely introduction to the art of cunnilingus. She licked and lapped, spurred on by the infinitesimal movements of the Princess's awakening body. The vine that penetrated Ellora was beginning to spear her in earnest now, in and out, harder and faster beneath Selina's lowered face. *Lucky Princess,* thought the tavern girl for a forgetful moment, *getting licked and fucked at the same time.* There was luxury indeed. The clit was big now, pulsing in Selina's mouth, slippery with juices. There was another precipitous loosening of the vines and a pair of legs thrashed about Selina's ears, accompanied by a very audible moan: the second coming.

Selina almost fell over into the swaying vines when rough

hands grabbed her from behind, lifted her skirt and yanked down her knickers.

"I don't know what you're up to, sweetheart, but it's making my blood burn," growled her assailant.

"Elrond! I just need to make her come one more time…"

"You do that." And then there was a hard, hot cock swarming up her from behind, encouraging her in her mission. "Make her come."

Selina, driven to addle-brained fever by the firm thrusting at her rear, plunged her mouth once more over the royal clitoris, bathing and laving, tickling and teasing. Elrond's fingers dug into her hips for purchase and he plowed her mercilessly while she licked. The grip of the vine was becoming ever more tenuous, whole sections slipping away and thudding to the ground. The Princess's body was flushed now, her chest heaving, her nipples tight. She began to twist her limbs and throw back her head against the bark, panting away. Only her closed eyes and the skewering action of the vines inside her sex conveyed her imprisonment now.

The pressure of Elrond's cock on Selina's G-spot threw her into her own undoing, her cries vibrating against Ellora's clitoris so that the Princess could no longer fight her third and biggest orgasm. Elrond, watching the two girls brought into rapture, released his own seed deep into Selina's willing darkness, then he leapt back in alarm as the Princess's eyes flew open and the vines snapped away, shrinking and shriveling until the entire plant dried into dust and disappeared.

A year and a day later, the Princess was married. Not to a gilded Princeling, chosen for her by her father, but to Selina. At the reception, August Villiers and the King fought a duel that proved fatal to the pair of them, and the Kingdom was thereafter ruled, fairly and wisely, by its joint Queens. Elrond continued to provide sterling service to his mistresses, and they all lived, as they deserved to do, happily ever after.

ELLIE AND THE SHOEMAKER

Louisa Harte

It was the end of summer and I needed a job. I'd been traveling for the past few months, but money had become tight. I saw an ad for a temporary assistant in a shoe store—the pay was good and it included free lodging, so I decided to check it out.

It wasn't what I expected. Tucked down a side street in a quiet part of town, the shop was small and unassuming. Still, the job had its perks—the owner for a start.

Tall and slim with dark glossy hair and a smart black suit, Jake was just my type. Up close he was even more attractive. As he showed me around the shop, his words went in one ear and out the other as I stared at his dark red lips, the cute mole on the left side of his nose and those gray-green eyes that sparkled when he smiled. He seemed shy though, as if he didn't realize just how sexy he was, and that made him more attractive.

The shop stocked a small range of shoes: simple, functional footwear that got a regular trade. The biggest surprise was that Jake made them all himself on the premises. I thought he was kidding until he led me to his workbench at the back of the shop for a demonstration. Donning a pair of studious black-framed glasses, he sat down on a stool and got to work. Sitting opposite, I watched as he cut and stitched the pieces of leather together to make a neat pair of shoes. Smart and sensible, the shoes weren't quite my style. But the guy was a natural. He took such care over making them: the intense look in his eyes, the passionate way he handled the leather...

It took all my effort to concentrate on the job. By the time he'd finished, I'd imagined him in at least six compromising positions, most of which included us naked on the workbench. Still, I reminded myself this was business not pleasure and managed to make a few sensible comments without betraying my feelings. After the demonstration, Jake took me upstairs to show me the room. Simple and sparse, it was all right, but I still couldn't take my eyes off Jake. He was so damn cute! I was sure from the way I was gawking at him he'd think I was a complete jerk.

But to my surprise, I was hired.

Next morning, the first thing Jake showed me was how to fit customers for shoes. Seating me on a stool, he slipped off my sandals. I was glad I was sitting down as my legs went all shaky when he touched me. Normally guys don't have this effect on me, but the way Jake held my foot and let his fingers play over my skin as he ran the measuring guide up against my toes turned me on. I tried to pay attention, but with him kneeling at my feet, his warm hands on my legs, I just wanted to ruck up my skirt and fuck him right there.

Fortunately, Jake was completely professional. If he sensed my lust, he didn't let on. He seemed far too busy for workplace distractions. He spent the rest of the day hunched over the bench turning out those smart, sensible shoes.

But my lustful thoughts wouldn't go away. Even after we

closed the shop and I went up to my room, I couldn't switch off. I just kept picturing Jake's slim fingers tucked into my knickers, his lithe body banging me over the wooden workbench. In the end I had to do something. Splayed out on the sofa in a skimpy robe, I closed my eyes and indulged my imagination. Sliding my hand between my thighs, I played with my pussy, trying to stifle the moans as I brought myself off.

I thought that should do it. But the next day, I still felt exactly the same. So I channeled my energy into serving the customers. What customers we had. They were few and far between. Still, Jake assured me he had his regulars, so I kept busy while Jake toiled away at the bench in the background. Then the telephone rang. Shadows passed over Jake's face as he answered it.

"I've got to go out," he said after he finished the call. "Will you be okay on your own, Ellie?"

Surprised, I nodded.

He didn't get back until late. He came in and went straight to his workbench and stared off into space.

"Is everything okay?" I asked.

Jake dropped his head, his gloriously glossy hair falling over his eyes as he answered. "Ellie, I'm broke."

That was it. In a second his world had come crashing down, mine with it. I'd only just started this job and I didn't want to lose it.

Seeing the concern on my face, Jake tried to sound hopeful. "Don't worry. I'm sure we'll get through it." But his voice sounded flat. Too tired to even think about sewing, he went upstairs to bed.

In a daze I went up to my room. The business was in trouble and yet he had still taken me on? I was touched. Curled up in my skimpy gown on the sofa, sipping a vodka, that's when I decided to help out. Perhaps it was a mix of alcohol and sexual frustration that made a night of sewing sound attractive, but regardless, I pulled my robe around me, crept downstairs and let myself into the shop.

Flicking on the light, I went over to Jake's workbench. On top of the bench were a few scraps of leather. This was likely his last batch of material. I paused as memories of high school sewing class flooded my mind—me sitting at the sewing machine trying not to feed it my fingers; Mum cringing at those crappy cushion covers I made; Dad's head engulfed in oversized sweaters and the hideous skirt I'd made to go out on the town that unraveled until it looked more like a belt. Still, this wasn't the time for doubt and gritting my teeth, I laid out Jake's tools and sat down to work.

At first I was awkward. I hadn't a clue what I was doing, but after a while I fell into a rhythm. My hands moved in a blur, as if some strange force had taken me over. It was like magic, something I couldn't explain, and within a few hours I'd finished.

I sat back and examined my creation. I had to admit I was impressed. By some strange freak of nature I'd made a really unique pair of shoes. Stylish and with a cute pointed toe, they were sassy. With a smile, I left the shoes in the middle of the bench and crept back upstairs to bed. I couldn't wait to see Jake's reaction.

Next morning, I went downstairs and opened up early. Jake walked in and did a double take. Walking over to the bench, he picked up the shoes. "What the..."

My stomach clenched as he studied them. I hoped I hadn't screwed up.

But turning to face me, Jake shot me a smile. "These are amazing—the stitching is so good, it looks like it's been done by an expert."

I basked in his praise.

But then he looked puzzled. "Where did they come from?"

Feeling coy, I dropped my gaze. "Perhaps you've got an admirer…"

Jake shook his head. God, he was sexy with that self-deprecating smile. Before he could ask any more awkward questions, I plucked the shoes from his hands and put them on display in the window.

"What are you doing?" he asked.

"Selling them of course."

To our delight, the shoes sold within an hour. Some rich woman came in and snapped them up, not batting an eye at the ridiculously high price I named. Jake went out and bought a colourful new batch of leather with the money, enough to make another two pairs of shoes. But on his return, he looked tense. "Ellie, what if people want more shoes like that?"

"Sleep on it, I'm sure something will work out," I offered.

"Yeah, okay. Why not," he said with a smile.

I couldn't believe it; Jake was loosening up. But I had a job to do and that night, I was at it again. Huddled at his workbench in my silky gown, I got to work. It was just like the previous night: as soon as I sat down at that bench, I went into a trance, my fingers deftly stitching like I was under a spell. This time I knocked out two pairs of shoes: a green pair with pink heels and a pair so black and shiny I could see my face in them. Kinky. Still, I wasn't gonna argue with my muse. I'd found my passion. Second to Jake, of course. The smile he'd given me was worth every minute hunched over his tatty workbench.

Next day, the shoes sold instantly. The buyers were awed, saying how "unique" and "exquisite" they were. I shrugged; there was no accounting for taste. But the price they paid was no joke and with the money Jake went straight out to buy more leather.

And so it went on. It became like a drug. I got high on Jake's increasing excitement. Every morning he came down earlier to see what surprises awaited him on the bench. After a while he even stopped asking questions. Perhaps a little part of him was starting to believe in his secret admirer. The shop became popular as its reputation spread. While Jake continued making shoes for his regular customers, I secretly worked by night turning out the crazy, funky designs. Together we were drawing crowds from miles around.

Those weren't the only changes. As the shop got busier, Jake spent less time at his workbench and more time with me. As I set up displays, he hovered behind me. Reveling in his attention, I let my skirt ride up to flash him my thighs, unbuttoned my blouse to show a bit of cleavage. From the look on his face, I was getting a reaction. But I was too afraid to act on it, too afraid to screw things up. If only Jake would make a move, transfer his passion from the workbench to me...

And then, a few weeks later, something wonderful happened. We were nominated for best shoe store in town. Despite the fact this was only a temporary position, I was surprised how much I cared—about the shoes, about the business.

About Jake.

After the nominations were announced, Jake became nervous and started asking awkward questions about the shoes. I reassured him and he seemed to relax. But just to be sure, in the days leading up to the judging, I worked so hard I hardly noticed the time; hardly heard the creak on the stairs—hardly noticed the shop door open and close behind me one night as I worked...

It was the night before the judging. I was sure we had enough shoes, but just to be safe, I tugged on my robe and crept downstairs to stitch one last pair. I opened the door. Under the soft lights, the shop looked amazing. While Jake had been out all day buying material, I'd been busy here, transforming the shop. I gazed around at the lavish displays, shelves of bright shoes and colorful banners, and I felt a knot tighten in my stomach; a hint of sadness that soon I'd be leaving. With a resigned sigh, I turned to the workbench to get down to work. And stopped.

There, in the center of the workbench stood a pair of killer red boots. In a daze, I walked over to the bench and picked them up. Slutty and sexy, they were right up my alley. With an excited giggle, I sat down on the stool and slid first one foot, then the other into the boots. Folding the leather around my legs I bent over to lace them up. They were a perfect fit! Thigh high and with a five-inch heel, they made my legs look amazing. Feeling horny and kinky, I leapt up off the stool and twirled around, gazing at myself in the shop mirror, my pussy growing wet at the sight of myself in my lusty attire.

Then I heard a noise—the door slowly opening. Clutching the robe to my chest, I turned around, my heart thumping.

A figure stood silhouetted in the doorway. "You found them," a voice said, so deep and husky I barely recognized it until the figure stepped into the light.

It was Jake.

Gone were the studious glasses and the prim dark suit, instead all he wore was a tight pair of jeans, a sexy smile and a look that could burn up the building.

I stood there, speechless. Realizing he was talking about the boots, I glanced down at them and then back up again. "Yeah, I mean...where did they—"

"Perhaps you've got an admirer..." The implication of his words glittered in his gray-green eyes.

"*You* made them for me?"

Slowly, Jake walked into the room, a mischievous smile on his face. "The other night, I heard a noise," he said. "So I came downstairs and opened the door. And what did I find...?"

His question echoed in the silence.

"My sexy assistant working her ass off in a flimsy little gown," he continued, not waiting for a reply. "That was some sight," he murmured. "So I thought I'd make her a pair she'd enjoy. Call it a thank-you..." Jake swept his gaze over my body. "And hell, they look good."

I shivered as he stalked toward me, a hungry look in his eyes. Brushing a curl from my face, he traced his finger over my cheek.

"What are you doing?" I whispered, surprised and delighted by this unusual show of dominance.

"Something I should have done ages ago..." Before I could respond, Jake grasped the belt of my gown and tugged. The belt slithered through its loops and came away in his hand. Sliding his fingers under the neckline of my gown, Jake pushed it off my shoulders.

I gasped as the robe fell to the floor. Apart from the boots, I was naked.

Jake exhaled as he stared at me. Curling his arms around my waist, he pulled me against him. My breasts flattened against his chest; my mound pressed hard against the front of his trousers. I moaned as he ran his fingers over my back, taking in the curve of my ass before scooping me up and carrying me to the workbench. Like a lover in a movie, he swept his hand over the wooden surface, sending materials clattering to the floor. Clearing a space, he lowered me down onto it.

Seeing this raw, primitive side of Jake made me wetter. I parted my thighs like a wanton slut. Instinctively, Jake stepped between them. I gasped as his huge, hard cock pressed against me through his trousers.

"Do the boots make you horny?"

"That and your cock against my pussy," I replied gamely.

With a satisfied smirk, Jake ground his hips against me, teasing me, coating the front of his jeans in my creamy excitement. I bit my lip. I was so damn horny I wanted to fuck him right then, but I knew that wasn't the way it would be. Jake wanted to take his time.

Pulling away slightly, he traced his hands over my breasts. My nipples hardened at his touch. Enjoying my arousal, Jake continued to play, teasing my nipples with his fingers and mouth. Releasing my tits, he moved his hand lower, down over my belly to the dark hair of my mound. I gasped as he slid his hand between my thighs. Running his hand over my slit, he swirled his fingers in my juice before lifting them to his mouth. "God, you taste good," he murmured, sliding first one finger then another between his dark red lips.

My clit throbbed with excitement at his words.

Sliding his hands over my thighs, he pushed my legs open wider. Then he dropped to his knees, my pussy level with his face. Watching me with those glittering eyes, he probed a finger into my cunt. I squirmed with delight, the rough edge of the bench digging into my butt as he drove his finger deeper. Then with a hungry moan, he buried his face in my pussy.

I cried out. I couldn't help it. Watching Jake's sleek glossy head bobbing between my thighs was so much better than my fantasies! I raked my hands through his hair as he laved my clit, tensed my toes in my boots as he fingered and sucked me. As his tongue moved faster, I ground my hips shamelessly. Jake looked up at me from between my thighs, his eyes intense, lusty.

Just what I'd been waiting for.

Gone was the shy guy with his smooth, steady exploration—now Jake was a man filled with need. Hauling himself to his feet, he tore at the front of his pants. But desire made him clumsy, and he swore as his fingers slipped off the buttons. Hungry to feel him inside me, I took over. I tugged open the buttons and pulled down his pants, letting the firm shiny head of his cock spring free. And what a cock! I slicked my hand up and down it, watching it lengthen and swell in my fingers. Pushing his pants to the floor, I shuffled to the edge of the bench and tilted my hips up toward him.

"Now fuck me..." I whispered.

Transformed with lust, the usually mild-mannered shoemaker didn't need asking twice. Cupping my butt in his hands, he slid his cock between my thighs and into my warm eager cunt. I moaned as he thrust his way in. My body tensed and I arched my back as he drove inside me. He moved slowly at first as if not wanting to hurt me, then thrust faster. The bench wobbled and creaked as we fucked. I squealed with pleasure as he impaled me, rocked against him, meeting his thrusts. I glanced in the mirror at our lusty liaison and smiled. It was the hottest display in the shop.

Jake's breathing became ragged. I could tell he was close. Slowing his rhythm, he pulled out of me, a questioning look in his eyes. An invitation for me to play?

I took it. Wearing the boots made me take charge. Time to show the boss who was *really* the boss.

Grabbing him by the shoulders, I marched him backward until he stumbled against a stool. He fell back onto it, his hard cock slick with my juice. With a smile, I straddled his hips. Jake groaned. He tongued my nipples as I sank down on his cock. I rode him with abandon, relishing the slick slap of our thighs as we slammed together on the stool.

My legs began to tremble. Rubbing my pussy up against him, I felt the orgasm building inside me. I couldn't hold out any longer. Jake caught my eye. It was as if he knew. With a wicked grin he grabbed my hips and pulled me down harder.

That was it—my pussy exploded. I cried out as convulsions shook my thighs. Watching me come on his lap, Jake's grin turned into a groan. Digging his fingers in my ass, he shot his load up inside me.

Panting, I leaned my head against Jake's neck, feeling a mix of emotions. Like pieces of leather, we fit together in more ways than one. The job couldn't go on forever; I'd known that from the start. But that didn't make me feel any better. I dipped my head. I wasn't going to cry. Not in front of Jake anyway.

Jake stroked his fingers through my hair. "Hey, Ellie?"

"Mmm?"

"Want to stay on?"

I lifted my head, anticipation fluttering in my belly. "What do you mean?"

"Be my partner…"

A smile bubbled on my lips. "Business or pleasure?"

Laughing, Jake ran his hands over my ass and gave me a squeeze. "Both."

Grinding my ass against him, I grinned. "Yeah, you're on."

We sealed the deal with a kiss. And a sleepless night of hot sex.

Six months later and I'm still here at the shop. We came second in the competition and since then, things have only gotten better. Now the shop's filled with customers, and Jake and I work together at the bench making all kinds of shoes.

Of course we always have fun testing them out first….

THE PUB OWNER'S DAUGHTER

Alegra Verde

The pub owner's daughter was a comely wench, fair of face and full of body. She was his only child. His wife had died in the birthing bed, but he loved his daughter no less for being the cause of it. She was his gift, one destined for joy and bounty, a girl child to care for him in his old age. When he tired of slinging grog, she would be his balm, his reward for a life spent serving up ale to wharf rats and hardened crooks. He need only keep her well and not cage her, as fathers were wont to do with their female children. An old woman had said as much on the eve of his daughter's birth.

Their lives were not unhappy. There was more than mopping up the slop left behind and lending ears to sad sods; there was laughter, and even camaraderie in the dank hole that they inhabited. However, the promise of a just reward while he yet breathed warmed him, and more, knowing that his only child would not end her days on the wharf lightened even his darkest days.

The old woman who blessed his daughter with the prophecy

had wandered in off the dock just as his wife was bearing down, the bed awash in red. There had been no physician or midwife. He hadn't been able to get one to venture into the stews that late at night, so he'd been glad to see the wizened face nearly hidden in the misshapen shawl. She was a woman and had to know more about these things than he did.

She had scooped the bloody babe up from between his wife's spent thighs and said, "Call her Treasure for she will bring you riches." She had stayed to clean and comfort his dying wife and had taught him how to prepare a sugar tit for the bawling babe. As he sat there cradling the suckling newborn, she'd said, "Don't hold her in. Let her have her head. She will find her way." She pressed her palm on the babe's abdomen, chanted words in a foreign tongue and said, "There, I've locked it. When it's opened properly, riches and true contentment shall be yours." With that, she wrapped the shapeless shawl around her head and shoulders and pressed past the blustery wind out into the darkness and pouring rain.

When Treasure became a woman and took her first lover, her father balked silently, but he neither admonished her nor killed the man, as he wanted to do. He remembered the old woman's words, "Let her have her head," and he bit his tongue and kept watch until the man, boots in hand, fumbled past him well before dawn.

He wondered if the old woman had meant it in this way. In all other things, Treasure was a good and dutiful daughter, perfectly malleable and respectful.

"Father," said Treasure, having shooed the man from her bed after his first effort and after rejecting even his most fervent pleas and promises to allow him a second chance. "There was no relief. I know there is more to this thing and I must find it."

It was then that she began her search. At the end of each

week, she would stroll through the pub in search of a likely man. If she found one that she fancied, she took him to her room and there they stayed until morning, the sound of their lovemaking ringing throughout the narrow taproom. The men who hadn't been chosen would suck on their mugs listening intently and longingly to the pounding headboard as it banged against the wall, the grunts and groans the lucky man made as he gave it his best and his cry of pleasure as he came long and hard. But, they never heard more than a mewl or a whimper from Treasure because she never came.

Before long, word spread that the pub owner's daughter, the comely Treasure, chose a man to bed at the end of every week from amongst her father's patrons. Men came from far and wide to be among the patrons on selection night. Some came earlier in the week hoping to attract her eye. Others brought gifts of cloth, flowers, fowl, spices and all manner of things that could be smuggled off the ships that lined the docks. One large dark-skinned man who wore a beard and a turban brought her a live lamb with a thick blue ribbon about its neck for a leash. She accepted the gift, as she graciously did all the other offerings, and gave him a kiss on his forehead, but she did not select him. He brought a full bolt of crimson silk the next week, but a thin fellow with almond eyes from the East was chosen.

She had no particular type. Tall, short, robust or pale, dark hair, no hair, she seemed to like them all. The only consistent factor was cleanliness. They had to be washed, an element that caused a run on the public bathhouses at week's end and improved the pub's air.

"It's not working," she said one night to her father as he counted coins. "In all these months, I have gained no relief."

"Daughter," he said. "This thing is of your choosing. If you choose not to continue, then so be it."

So for the next few weeks Treasure served ale, flirted with many men who grinned up at her, and even joined in their bawdy songs, but she did not choose one to take upstairs to her bed.

Soon word got around, as it often does, that none of the men on which she had bestowed her favors had pleased her. The men grumbled about this amongst themselves, each assuring the other or the room at large that he was the one to please her. They boasted to each other and sometimes, after a few drinks, to her of their prowess, claiming to have uncanny abilities with their tongues or fingers. One old man promised a delight with his toes that he had learned in his travels to uncharted parts of Asia. More often than not, they padded their codpieces claiming to have an appendage the size of which she had never seen or felt. They would stroke themselves and she would smile, nod and slide their newly filled mugs onto the table before slipping away.

One day the woman in the misshapen shawl appeared. She found a bench in a corner and when Treasure approached she bade her sit with her for a moment. And Treasure, who never sat with the customers, slid easily onto the bench beside the woman.

The old woman began, "I attended your birth and washed your mother before she was put into the ground. I promised her that I would help you find what you needed in this world." She patted Treasure's arm. "Tell me child. How do you fare?"

Treasure looked at the woman whose warm eyes soothed and suddenly feeling no shame, spoke freely. "I lust after men but can find no relief. For long months, I have chosen a man each week and taken him to my bed but have found no release."

"How have you chosen these men?"

"In the beginning I chose men who were fair of face with full heads of hair that smiled on me with laughter in their eyes.

"They were always eager and before we reached the top of

the stairs their appendage would be at full tilt. Within seconds, I'd be on my back, my skirts over my head, and they would be shouting their relief while I lay wet and sticky.

"I tried the beefy ones next. Some had big cocks, others not so. Some wanted to ride me until dawn. Others were like the pretty ones, quick and messy.

"The small wiry ones were more inventive. They liked to suckle my breasts and some placed kisses on my sex. One licked and kissed my sex for hours before producing a leather-clad faux appendage. He confessed that he was a eunuch and because he had no sac was unable to obtain an erection. However, he assured me he had pleasured many women when he served in the harem. Alas, I found no relief through his ministrations though he tried well into the wee hours."

"You must not give up child," the old woman said patting Treasure's hand. "You will know relief...and joy. I promise you this. This time is for learning the ways of men, for weeding out the chaff, for discovering what you truly need."

"If you say so, mistress."

"Soon child, soon." With that, the woman took her leave.

To the joy of her father's patrons, Treasure chose a man that week. He was a ship's captain, tall and agile, and proved to be a measured and methodical lover.

He undressed her slowly, then himself so that she could feast on the beauty of his lean body and the perfection of his aroused penis. He sucked at her breasts, each in its turn, leaving the nipples tight and wet and slightly chilled. Then he feasted on the rest of her body, his lips and tongue nipping and sucking at her resilient skin, teasing her inner thighs with the tip of his tongue, and pulling the sensitive labia into his mouth with gently applied teeth.

When he took her, it was sharp and hard. His sex, like a

well-directed battering ram, pushed through her tight, moist opening to find itself well entrenched in the heat of moist flesh. He seemed lost in her body, his eyes closed, his lips pressed tight as he moved.

"Treasure," he groaned her name as he rode her. "Treasure." She held on, her hand at his shoulders, her eyes watching him, and it was good, better than it had ever been, but she found no relief.

When he came, filling her with his relief, she held him and let him shower her face with kisses. He pulled her to him, her back to his front and they slept like that for a while, but when he asked if he could come again she told him no.

She took a few more lovers after the captain, but none neared the pleasure she felt with him and none brought her relief. She considered that maybe she'd made a mistake not having invited the captain back. Maybe he warranted a second try. But some instinct told her to stay her course. He had not been the first to vie for more. Several, having found pleasure with her, had offered, nay demanded, that she leave this life and make one with them. They would not hold her past against her, they vowed. One had tried to spirit her away in the night and her father, who always guarded her more diligently on selection night, had to use the cudgel he kept in his pocket for unruly customers. No, men were territorial and she couldn't risk it with the captain. The old woman had promised that she would find relief. She must continue her journey.

This night she chose a man of maybe five and thirty. She had noticed him before but had never selected him because he always sat in the corner watching her, watching everyone. He seemed somehow troubled, almost fearful, and spoke only occasionally to her father. Her father seemed to like him, leaning in from time to time to laugh and share a word as he refilled his mug.

This day, however, he sat at a bench near the front of the room. He was clean and well dressed as usual, his linen sparkling white against his sun-darkened skin.

"What'll you have?" she asked, knowing the response before it was given.

"You, tonight, if you'll have me." His voice was soft and warm, the words lacking the brashness with which they were usually delivered.

"An old line, sir."

"And yet still heartfelt." His eyes too were warm and soft.

"Is that why you've moved to the center of things? I thought you had an unnatural fondness for my father."

He laughed. "No. I was afraid."

That admission surprised her. She took a moment to consider her response.

"Of me?"

He nodded.

"Why?"

He was silent. She leaned in to hear him better.

"You are so alive in this thing. You wield your power so completely. I am awed."

She smiled and kissed him on the side of his mouth. He flinched.

"I shall have you tonight," she said as she straightened. "Ale?"

He nodded.

"That one," she said to her father as she pointed to the solitary man. "I'll have that one this week."

"Good choice, daughter. He has waited long to muster the courage. He seems a good enough man. Maybe he'll give you your relief."

"Aye," she said, nodding at her father's word, but sadly, as she had little hope. This one was pleasant enough, but not unlike the many others in appearance.

At the appointed time, she went to the sun-darkened man and bade him come with her. The others looked on hungrily. Some whooped loudly and made catcalls, but none objected as the process was long understood and accepted.

When they entered the room, he stood meekly in its center, fully clothed and waiting.

"Well?" she asked.

He looked up at her questioning.

"Undress."

"Everything?"

She nodded realizing that she wanted him unclothed. She wanted to see his body, to touch it.

Sliding the small buttons from beneath the loops that ran the length of her bodice, she watched as he unfastened and removed the black leather jerkin then began to pull the shirt over his head to reveal a broad chest with a spray of dark hair just at the center. The muscles of her sex clenched and she moved toward him. He looked at her warily and even took a step back, his arms still caught in the sleeves of his shirt.

She lowered her mouth to the darkly pebbled flat nipples on his chest and sucked. Her tongue toyed with the coarse hair that surrounded them. She licked the tiny nipples again coaxing them to rise. He groaned, his hands and arms still high over his head tangled in his shirt.

She pushed him back. He stumbled a bit until the back of his knees touched the mattress and he tumbled backward. She didn't know what had come over her, but she felt fevered. Her puss twitched and she could feel the moisture running down her thighs. She never wore undergarments on selection night so there was no linen chemise or drawers to collect her rampant juices.

He wiggled a bit, struggling with the shirt.

"Be still," she ordered and he stilled.

She stood over him looking her fill. Her bodice was splayed open and her breasts sat up high peeking out of the thickly embroidered cloth. They were full and free and buoyant, the nipples aroused, long and aimed at their prey. She felt his eyes on her and her puss twitched again, the muscles tightening in expectation.

"Don't move," she said. "Don't try to touch me. If you do, I'll call my father and he'll toss you out. Do you understand?"

He nodded. In his eyes, fear warred with anticipation.

Kneeling on the floor beside him, she slowly loosened his codpiece and unbuttoned his hose, her fingers grazing his sex through the thick-paned wool. He was hot and hard and he jumped each time she touched him. She reached over, and with both hands, pulled his hose, codpiece and all, over his hips and down around his knees. His cock sprang out, full and long, solid and dusky like the rest of him. A nest of dark coarse hair framed his sex and his sac. Standing up, she surveyed her feast. He lay there, his arms still tangled in the stark white linen, much of which trailed down to frame his thick locks and pleasant face. His broad chest with its hair-dusted tabs and the narrow waist gave way to his rampant sex and taut thighs. He shifted his booted feet, the leather crackling as his legs rubbed restlessly against the footboard.

She moved between his open legs and lowered her mouth, closing it over his sex. The bulbous head filled her mouth, its shape and salty tang making her want to suck and slurp at it like the spoon when she made syllabub. She sucked and he moved restlessly beneath her moaning his pleasure. Her hands found the firm cheeks of his bottom and squeezed, relishing the sleekness and resilience of skin and muscle. He bucked beneath her, pressing himself farther into her mouth.

She took her mouth away and, pinching a bottom cheek, she spoke to him as though he were a recalcitrant servant. "Don't move or there will be no relief. Remain as you are until you are given permission to do otherwise."

Cowed, he looked down the bed at her and nodded, his hardened cock throbbing in agreement. She resumed sucking, enjoying the width and heat and flavor as it filled her mouth and the rasp of its various textures as it slid in and out. He squirmed, his thighs tightening as he continued to swell. Soon his size strained her mouth, and he was writhing on the bed, trying to keep from thrusting upward and barely able to contain himself.

Only then did she gather her skirts and straddle him. Her wet sex pressed into his groin. His crazed cock pressed into the crevice of her buttocks.

He watched her, his eyes devouring her breasts. She rasped her sex against the coarse hair of his groin. It tingled. She rubbed herself against it again, a lazy cat scratching an itch. The hard flesh of his sex wedged tight between her cheeks began a slow slide up and down.

She stopped, pulling herself from the growing pleasure, opened her eyes and glared down at him. Fear rounded his eyes. He closed them but only for a moment. His eyes sought hers, soft and pleading. His arms strained up toward the headboard.

She leaned forward, pressing her buoyant breasts into the hardened muscles of his chest, her nipples denting the flesh. Finding the pillow softness of his lower lip, she bit down. He groaned, his mouth seeking hers. Hers refused, nipping him again then using her tongue to lave the stinging lips.

He was breathing hard now, panting.

She rose up, nipped a shoulder, a nipple. Her tiny teeth found the tough skin at his rib cage. He writhed beneath her, moisture dripped from his sex and coated the crevice between her cheeks.

"Please," he begged, his arms straining upward, his riding boots scuffing against the footboard.

"Please," he cried. She nipped another shoulder, harder this time, and he bucked beneath her. His eyes were shut tight and his teeth sank into his lower lip.

Gathering her skirts higher, she rose and watched as she sank down onto his swollen sex. He made a grateful noise of contentment as her flesh swallowed his. She squeezed, causing her muscles to grasp at his eager appendage, but she had liked the way his girth pierced her, the way it had pressed its way in creating a rasping friction as it made its way up her channel to create a resonating bounce at her center. She rose and did it again and again until her whole body was wound so tight that she couldn't think. His cries of pleasure coming from deep in his throat somehow penetrated her thoughts, and she moved her hand up to cover his mouth, to silence him.

Unbalanced by the movement, she found herself sprawled atop him, his appendage lodged at a strangely pleasant angle. She pressed backward, his sex rasping against an uncharted spot. A jolt of lightning flared deep inside her. She tried it again. Her breasts tingled as they rubbed against the hair of his chest. The lightening flared again and he cried out.

Driven now, she pressed backward in earnest, a rhythm claiming her as the warmth grew and spread with each backward thrust. He was saying something or making a noise deep in his throat as he thrust upward, but she didn't stop to chastise him because it felt too good and the light and warmth was growing.

Suddenly, she felt him hardening inside her, stronger than any appendage she had ever felt. She pressed back and he thrust forward. Back and forward they rocked and pressed and butted against each other until the lightning consumed them, the dam burst and they collapsed semiconscious into a heap of melded flesh.

Sometime after dawn, their flesh cooled and they were able to disentangle themselves, wash and dress. He kissed her forehead as he left, but he never offered his name nor did she ask.

Before the week was near an end, a large chest filled with silks, spices and jewels arrived with a note thanking her for "a memorable evening and an experience unsurpassed."

It was unsigned and left no hint as to how the benefactor might be contacted. But what did it matter? She had no desire to become territorial. She had found her relief, and it had been all that she had dreamed. Now she could move on with her life. She considered selling some of the jewels and buying a small house in town, maybe a flower or milliner's shop. There was more than enough. Her father thought it a grand idea and encouraged her to do so.

Although she would have denied it, the hope that the man would return kept her rooted in place. She waited tables, flirted with the customers, even joined in their bawdy songs, but she never took another man to her room.

Months passed and business was still good because many hoped that Treasure would renew her Selection Day trysts. Even if she didn't, she was still a treat for the eyes and pleasant company. Further, the grog had suddenly become more potent. Rumor was that the barkeep had come into a recent windfall and diluting his spirits with less water was his way of celebrating and sharing his good fortune with his customers.

The man who had given her relief rolled in on a blustery

night. Taking his old place in the far corner of the bar, he ordered his ale and took up his watch.

His cape whirled about him as he pushed through the heavy wooden door. She had seen him as he'd come in, but she'd not acknowledged him, not wanting him to think her territorial. Although that was what she was feeling. Yes, that and rage. Where had he been? Why had he not come for her? When she could stand it no longer, she made her way across the room, planted her feet in front of him and wrapped her arms across her chest.

"Well?"

"Good evening, Treasure," he said as if nothing more than the tipping of a hat had occurred between them.

"And to you, sir. However, I find it off putting that you know my name and where I reside and I know nothing of you."

"I am Leland Nash of Devonshire."

"So Leland Nash, why have you stayed away?"

"I am please to learn that you took notice of my absence."

"You gave me relief and I would have you again...to see if the effect can be recreated."

"I was told that you granted each man only one audience. I was afraid to hope. So I stayed away."

"You have cause to hope. Mind you, I am making no claim. I am not one to mark my territory as men do."

"I would not mind," he said to his ale rather than to her.

"Well, I am not one to do so. It's just that you are the only one who has been able to assist me in finding relief and I would like to do so again."

He looked at her then, his eyes searching hers. "It is thus with me, also." He leaned forward so that only she could hear. "My member had often remained flaccid when I attempted involvement, and when a woman did excite me to arousal I

could give her pleasure until she was beyond sated, but I could
never achieve relief. It was my mother, you see."

"Your mother?" she asked.

"No really, it was my father."

"Your father?" she repeated his words.

"Yes, he was a philanderer and never returned the love and
fidelity my mother gave him. He died as he came into a whore
he had pressed against a wall. It took two coachmen to free the
poor woman. My mother was inconsolable and in a fit of rage,
she cursed her unborn son saying that 'he should achieve relief
only with his true love.'

"I had determined to remain celibate and would have joined
a seminary if I hadn't been my father's heir and only son. A few
months ago, I came upon an old woman huddled in a doorway
as I made my way back to my rooms. I gave her a few coins to
get food and maybe a warm place to sleep for the night. Grateful,
she clutched my hand and said in a most soothing voice that
what I sought was here." He made a broad gesture that encom-
passed the entire pub.

"So I came here and saw you. I watched and waited, but it
seemed impossible."

She leaned forward and nipped his bottom lip. He smiled and
licked the tingling spot.

The pub owner's daughter no longer lives over the pub and
Selection Day is only the well-embellished memory of the pub's
patrons. She and her husband live with their three children and
his mother in Devonshire where he manages his family's proper-
ties. They are well and happy and she and her husband often
take time to hole up in their chambers while Leland lets his wife
have her way with him and they find relief together.

SLEEP TIGHT

Janine Ashbless

The house, built of red brick, is Victorian by the look of it, with fancy piecework tiles all along the ridges of the complex roofline. It's called the Gables, which is appropriate because that's just about all anyone can see of it over the bramble thicket that clogs the whole garden. It's been a decade since anyone last cut that. Do you have *any* idea how much bramble can grow in ten years? Some of those stems are fatter than my thumb, and the thicket stands about seven feet tall, pressing through the iron railings and sending out snaky tendrils to catch the hair of passersby on the street. The route to the front door is absolutely impassable. At least they won't have had to worry about squatters getting in.

Ten years. You'd think people with that sort of money would have more sense. The whole place has just been abandoned.

"Access up to the house and right round the walls," that cold little lawyer guy said when we stood on the front pavement together and eyeballed the wall of stems. They needed to do a structural survey every ten years, he explained, just to make sure the building was still sound.

"If I clear the whole lot you'll find it loads easier to sell," I offered. "It'd take me, oh…three, four days—it's a big garden. Including removal of the brush, obviously."

"The house isn't up for sale, Mr. Risborough. We're simply entrusted with its upkeep."

With a shrug I quoted him for a day's work: that was all I estimated it would take to cut a path through to the front door and around the building. He didn't even try to bargain me down. So that was how it worked out. And here I am on a hot summer morning, my truck parked up in front of the gate, getting the brushcutter out of the back and filling its tank with two-stroke.

I feel good; I'm looking forward to a day's work, to the powerful heft of the cutter under my hands, to seeing the bramble's defenses fall before me. The harness goes over my faded Aerosmith T-shirt and the hook sits over my right hip so the brushcutter's weight hangs comfortably, the cutting head swinging just above the tarmac. The band of my plastic helmet is already making my forehead sweat. My thick leather gloves grip the handles. Steel-toed boots and a pair of old chainsaw chaps make up the rest of my gear: they look a bit like cowboy chaps but beneath the blue fabric they're filled with nylon padding. I'm not wearing them for fear of the cutter head but because I don't want my jeans shredded by the thorns. It's too warm to wear coveralls.

The engine purrs like a tiger. Down goes the mesh visor of my helmet, *efff* go my ear-protectors as they settle into place, cutting off the outside world. All I'm aware of now is the silver shaft of my cutter, the triskelion of dark blades and the mass of interlaced shrubbery in front of me. The familiar smell of gas fumes burns my nose.

It's just about possible to see the line of the path cut last time:

the bramble rises a few inches less high, the stems are a little less thick though still hard and woody. Only the top surface of the mass is green and leafy, and right now it's dotted with white flower heads. Everything below that layer is pure pain, the thorns curved like teeth. There's only one way to tackle such a tangle: I lift the head of the cutter like it's a four-foot hard-on jutting from my pelvis, squeeze the trigger till the blades sing and lower it onto the bramble from above. Stems shred. The whole thicket quivers. The weighted head falls, slow-mo, clearing a narrow slice through the biomass.

Up, down. Up, down.

It's straightforward work but satisfying enough. No grave-stones or baby trees to worry about avoiding on this site at least. A fine mulch of vegetable matter soon dusts me from toe to throat but thankfully—unlike plenty of places I've worked—it doesn't include any dog shit. If only if wasn't so hot it'd be easy. What is it with the weather this year? Global warming, like they say? One day pissing rain, the next fiercely hot: Scotland to the Med in twenty-four hours. I'm glad I'm not working indoors.

It takes me all morning to even approach the house, clearing a two-yard path. I hardly notice, measuring the time only by the regular refills of my gas tank. I'm off in my own little world, thinking over stuff while my body carries on: supplies to pick up, an advert to go in the local free magazine, the tax form to fill in before October. My sandwiches get eaten in the cab of my truck, the radio tuned to a station playing halfway decent stuff from the eighties. Then I pick up my voice mail. Among a scattering of customer enquiries I'll deal with tonight is a message from Charlene: *Whoa! Just got up—You should have been there last night. It was wild! Miss you, lover. I'll phone tonight for a proper chat, yeah?*

I smile. Charlene's in Ibiza, partying to the max with her

girly mates. I could have been there, too, but there's just too much work in my line of business come summer. I wonder what they've been up to and think it's probably best I don't know. I'm looking forward to hearing her voice tonight though: a "proper chat" means a bit of dirty talk and some long distance sexplay. I'm already imagining her whispered words, the luxury of settling back on the sofa and listening to her breathy giggles growing sharper and her responses more broken as I describe all the things I'd like to be doing to her, while my right hand leisurely stokes my imagination.

Jeez. My cock's already filling out impatiently: there's a firm bulge growing in my denims. It must be the heat. And I do miss Charlene, even after only a few days: the soft small body in the bed beside me, the smell of her hair, the way she wriggles joyfully under my casual caress. I give myself a brief squeeze, promising more tonight, and climb out of the cab to start the afternoon shift.

It takes another hour to reach the house and get a good start on clearing a perimeter strip. It's the hottest part of the day now. The brickwork is the color of dried blood and reflects the heat back at me; there's not a breath of air down here with the bricks on one side and the wall of thorns on the other. There are wild roses growing among the brambles, I notice, their falling petals as pink as my Charlene's nipples. The smell of roses and mulched greenery is almost choking. My feet crunch the big dried stems underfoot. The ground floor windows are boarded up, I see, though in a few places the boards have rotted or slipped and the bramble stems have tried to climb into the house though the gaps.

The strimmer roars louder as it hits fumes at the bottom of the empty petrol tank, and then the engine cuts. I push my visor up and cock the pads over my ears back, grateful for even those slivers of cool air on my skin. My shirt is stuck to my back and my arms are covered in scratches; I wonder why bramble scratches always burn like that. Lifting the shaft of the cutter erect I turn in that narrow space and trudge back toward the porch where I've left the petrol can.

But while I'm crouched over, refueling, my eye falls on the porch. It was filled with long thorny whips of bramble of course, until I came along and chopped the lot into splinters. Plenty of severed stems still hang from the angles of the peeling woodwork though. Leaving the brushcutter where it lies, I get up and start clearing these tendrils away, folding the cruel ropes into shorter lengths and throwing them aside. It makes a change from strimming, just for a few moments.

That's when I finally notice that the front door is ajar; only by a finger's-breadth, but the line of darkness seizes my eye. I feel a twinge of concern that's close to annoyance; if the place wasn't locked up properly last time then I've just demolished its only line of defense, and I don't want to be held responsible if it gets burgled or torched. Then a flutter of curiosity rises to the fore. Putting my hand on the wooden door, I give it a gentle push. Paint flakes off under my hand, but the door swings stiffly open a little way.

It looks temptingly shadowy in there. I've been out in the sun all day, and my jeans are clinging to my legs with sweat. Quietly, I step over the threshold into the blessed shade.

It takes a minute for my eyes to adjust to the gloom. I focus on the tiled floor first: leaves have blown in over the years and made little heaps, but they've progressed no farther than the bottom of the stairs, which still boasts a carpet of an indeterminate murky color. The place smells a little damp, but I've known worse. I look round, but there's no light switch in sight on the wall—not, of course, as I remind myself, that the electricity would still be on. No switches and no sockets and no light-fitting overhead. I wonder how long it has been since this place was inhabited.

I should go. I've no business in here, despite enjoying the relief the shade offers. What stops me leaving is a sound.

Running water.

I lick my parched lips. I've got a flask of tea back at the van and a third of a plastic bottle of water left over from my pack-up dinner. That thought's not nearly so compelling as the trickle of liquid coming from inside the house. Somewhere on ground level, I think, turning my head. Somewhere toward the back of the house.

I open the door wider to admit more light before stepping carefully down the hall and turning into a large back room. There's some light in here, too; directly opposite me is a sash window. The upper half has slid down—presumably the cords have rotted—and the topmost board nailed to the frame beyond has vanished, allowing a narrow wedge of light to enter and diffuse through the damp air. Severed bramble cords droop into the room. Directly under the window is a big stone sink with a single tap. That's where the sound is coming from. My eyes are still adjusting to the gloom but I get the impression of benches around the wall and white tiles. It's a kitchen, obviously. Approaching the sink I strip off one glove and poke my finger cautiously under the tap. The flow is wonderfully cool. I lift the finger to give it a sniff, but it doesn't smell stagnant or anything. I taste the drips with the tip of my tongue.

It's just water. It's running out of the wide bronze mouth of the tap at a steady rate. I can't help wondering how long it's been flowing. Let's hope they're not paying for this on a water meter.

My helmet goes off and on the floor. Both gloves go inside it and I wash my hands, splashing the water up to my elbows, making the bramble scratches sting. It's cold on my skin, bloody lovely. I dump my harness with a click and a shrug, then pull off my T-shirt and soak it under the tap; wringing it out I swab down my bare chest and throat. My skin thrills; I don't think I realized how uncomfortable I was in the heat until now. Slinging the wet shirt over one shoulder I cup my hands—careful not to touch anything, mind—and take a drink. Afterward I grope for the tap, but it's too stiff to turn and I don't try to force it closed.

Only when I turn away do I realize how much more of my surroundings are visible. It's definitely a kitchen; there are pots hanging off hooks and a laundry creel like my gran used to have overhead. In the middle of the room, though, there's a bed with a curved wooden headboard. And on the bed there's a body.

In a split second my own body goes from too hot to so cold I'm frozen in place. I feel the gather of sweat at the small of my back form a slow trickle that slides down under the waistband of my jeans like a chilled fingertip. I hear the sound of my voice, echoing a little as an expletive falls from my lips.

It's a body. I can make that out clearly; it's pale against the dark bedding, slim, a woman or a kid. My head swims. All I can think, bizarrely, is that I've been drinking out of a tap in a room with a corpse. Why the hell didn't I notice it? How come I didn't smell the thing?

Because there is no smell. This room isn't even as musty as the hall. There's no hint of an odor, except the faintest smell of wild roses and wet stone. I look back to the kitchen door and the hall beyond. My mobile is locked up in the van. I'm going to have to call the police. And then tell them why I was in here to find the corpse. The day's just turned to shite.

I need to be sure. I'm having problems believing even my own eyes in this light. Inch by inch I shuffle across the flagstones, holding my breath, until I'm close enough to get a proper look.

It's a young woman. She looks perfect. Her hands are resting neatly on her torso about at the level of her diaphragm. Her bare feet point at the ceiling. Her head floats in a sea of long dark hair and she has dark brows. I can't begin to guess what she's doing laid out in the kitchen of a deserted house. How long has she been left here?

Then I see the soft rise and fall of her breastbone, and I realize she's not dead after all, and the relief is so immense I feel drunk.

"Ah—hello?" My voice is hoarse. The scene makes no more sense now of course: what's she doing sleeping in this place? If she's a squatter, how on earth did she get in? The only means of entrance I can imagine to the Gables involves a helicopter and a skylight. "Hello?"

She doesn't stir. I edge closer. Before I reach out I make very, very sure that I can see her breathing, that it wasn't just a trick of my eyes. She's wearing a long dress of gray lace that doesn't really hide that much of the pale body beneath. I can see the peaceful expression on her pointed little face. I can see the curves of her waist and hips and thighs. I can see her breasts, flattened a little by gravity but embarrassingly distracting still. They rise and fall slowly and for a moment I'm mesmerized. Black and sticky thoughts crawl in my skull before I shrug them off.

Gingerly I touch her shoulder. "Hey?"

No response. Her flesh feels cool but not cold.

Stoned, I think. Or drunk. She'd have heard me otherwise. Grasping the curve of her shoulder more firmly, I give her a little shake. "You okay?"

She doesn't answer. All that happens is that her breathing deepens audibly, and the lace catches on my calloused hand and shreds as I lift it. The lace is actually rotten; the threads fall almost into dust. I blink stupidly. Then I reach over to take her by both shoulders and I shake her harder, lifting her an inch from her bed. She falls back upon the dark velvet coverlet with a sigh, and as I withdraw I somehow manage to snag the garment across her breast and tear it open; it offers no more resistance than cobweb.

Fuck, I think witlessly. And I see that where the fabric has pulled and torn across the sweet pale curve of her right breast, her nipple has responded to the stimulus. As I watch, it hardens visibly, rising like a pale pink bud from its areola. I watch as my fingers steal back to brush that swelling mound and it stiffens to dimples.

My head is spinning. This is all like a dream. It can't be real. There can't be a young woman asleep in a house that's been locked up for ten years. She can't be impossible to wake. I can't be watching my fingertips touch her—softly, so softly—so that the cushion of her breast is topped by a flushed pearl. I can't be hearing a gentle moan in her throat.

For a moment I think she's woken, and I withdraw my hand an inch. She arches a little as if in pursuit of my touch, her breasts rising. Then she relaxes with a ghostly whimper of loss.

It's like a dream, or a story. An old, familiar story. I moisten my dry lips, knowing what I need to do. Gently I sit on the bed—it's actually a horsehair couch and almost unyielding—and I lean forward to kiss her. She has full, provocative lips for such otherwise delicate features. They feel cool under mine.

But all she does is smile in her sleep, faintly.

A second time I bend to kiss her, and this time I cup both her breasts, feeling their soft mounds yield beneath my hot hands. She's as cool as earth and as velvety as a flower petal and she tastes of rosewater. I tug at her nipples until they're both stiff like beads. I hear her whimper.

Then I sit back. Nothing has changed: her eyes are still shut, their dark lashes etched on her pale cheeks. I'm awash with confusion and shame and arousal. Under my jeans my cock is kicking angrily at its confines, swollen with selfish need. Her pale breasts shine through the shreds of her garment like moons rising through clouds. Without letting myself think I run a fingertip down the length of her body, tearing a furrow through the old gray lace. *If it's so fragile,* a part of my mind asks, *how did she put it on?*—but I ignore the question. She's just too much of a temptation. I reach the slight swell of her pubic mound and slide my fingers under and through the lace, cupping her.

She's hairless, peachy, as soft and cool as mounded flour. No stubble. Just velvet petals of flesh hiding a liquid heart, and as I squeeze softly her hips tilt, pushing her sex up against my fingers. Her head tilts back a little and her lips part as she breathes a hungry moan. I nod as if answering a question and curve my fingers in, searching deeper. She's wet, though surprisingly cool still. I can smell the intoxicating sharp musk of her sex now. It's on my fingers. My fingers are stroking up and down that furrow, finding the source of the wet, finding the stud of her clit. I like frigging Charlene; I'm good at it; this is easy.

That memory of Charlene is as insubstantial as old lace, a thing belonging to the sunlit world. This girl's body, the stretch of her throat as she tilts her head back and the sharp rise of her breasts, the satin slipperiness under my hand—they're all that count in this twilit dream. She's extraordinarily responsive to my touch, as if she's waited a hundred years for this. Maybe she has. I can see the shudder of her hips, the tautness of her flat belly as I stroke her, a single finger making her dance. I can see her fingers flex and pull at her own flesh but she doesn't open her eyes; her questing is blind. She needs me. She needs the hand that's working between her thighs.

She's close to coming.

And my other hand goes to uncinch my belt buckle, unzip and reach into my jeans. My cock bounces free, scorching hot against my palm. I'm aching for release. I swear I only mean to touch myself, to jack off as I watch her climax. But without thinking I find myself climbing on the bed, kneeling over her, parting those slim thighs without regard to the tearing of the lace, slipping into that wet furrow like into a pool of clear water, quenching my burning cock in her cool grip. She's exquisite. My thrusts are deep but slow as, dream dizzy, I savor each moment and each move.

I feel her arch beneath me, and I hear her plaintive little moans turn to gasps. I feel the shift of her hips as she lifts her legs and digs her heels into my ass, pulling me in deeper. Her arms furl about my neck. And then I start to ride her faster as the lead in my balls turns molten and starts to rise, as that tight grip clenches and I hear the unmistakable quivering cry of her orgasm.

She opens her eyes and smiles at me. Her eyes are dark, without reflection.

I'm right on the edge. Nothing's going to stop me coming now, not even the sight of her teeth as she peels back full lips to reveal fangs like a snake's that she sinks deep into my throat.

Not even that.

I come and come and come, and I scream as I do. But there's a bit of me that isn't shocked at all.

I mean, what else can sleep for a hundred years?

HER HAIR IS A NET, WOVEN

Shanna Germain

When he sees her at the market, although he knows what and who she is, he wants her anyway. He always wants her. It's her face that catches him first, as it often does, makes his gaze focus and puts that steady beat in his breastbone. She half turns and there it is: her pale face, round and unlined as a rivered stone, as the year's first full moon, its circle caught against the dark sky of her straight, wet hair. The sight of her washes over and through him, a tight pressure in his head that he can't shake.

She's not buying anything. She's watching the baby chicks cluck and fluff in their cages; putting a lean finger to the curled side of a cabbage covered in dew; canting her head at the puppeteer playing his wooden figures for the flock of children.

He knows he shouldn't go to her, not here, but she draws him in without meaning to, the way the sea calls to sailors. He moves himself to stand behind her, not close enough to touch, but close enough that he can see the dampened hem of her pale green skirt. Close enough to see the bits of algae and water bugs and roe caught in the tide of the fabric as it rises and ebbs around her bare feet. Her hair is long and black, smooth as glass or ice. He wants to fist his hands around the length of it and pull it upward to his nose, inhale the brackish, living smell of her. Instead, he watches her watch the puppet man, each of his wooden figures caught on the end of a string, moving up and down, striding and speaking at the manipulator's command. She doesn't laugh or smile. Her expression rests in the shift of her hips, in the soft wiggle of her fingers as they flutter against her face.

He says her name three times. This, he knows, is how you catch the daughter of a waterman.

Once, at the place he stands.

Again, a step forward.

Third, as he touches two fingers to the side of her waist, feeling the gauzy fabric and the curve of her hip shimmy and flow beneath his hand as he captures her.

She doesn't make a noise or step away. She barely moves. Only the dress shifts as she leans back to rest against his chest, the fabric parting to expose the smoothed inner curves of her breasts, the cool length of her neck.

"What are you doing here," he asks in her ear. He swears he can hear the liquid slide through her veins at the side of her neck, crystalline pulses beneath her pale skin.

"Buying butter." Her voice catches the water in the wind and shakes it out like tiny droplets. "What am I always doing here?"

There is no butter in her hands. He wonders what omens that might signal. The tales tell of the waterman's daughter: when she buys high, the markets flood like spring rivers. Low, and everything dries up, hard and hurtful. What, he wonders, does it signify, when she doesn't buy anything at all?

He brushes his palm up the side of her hip, the place where the swell crests over the bone. "Where are your red stockings? I almost didn't recognize you."

They both know this is a lie.

"Those are not for you," she says, and there is flint in her voice.

He feels ashamed for his tease but doesn't apologize. She says she doesn't believe in those kinds of things.

"Besides, you are supposed to accidentally come upon me bathing naked." She leans back to rest against his chest and as she half turns, her eyes are blue-black, so deep there is no end. *A man could drown in those eyes,* he thinks, but he doesn't say so. He can't imagine how many men have said that to her. How many times she's shaken their words away. "Down by Rigley's well."

"I accidentally came upon you last time," he says, the tease in his voice taking on a playful heat, a catch of double wording that he can't resist, caught as it is inside the memory of their last time, the way her cool, thin fingers had eddied around him and teased him into coming, his heat splashing on the shore of her skin.

She doesn't take the bait, though, merely looks at him. He winces—there's something in that look that reminds him how ancient she is, how many men she's probably seen who fawn over her and pull at her hem like children. He wants her. He loves her; the thought comes to him unbidden, but he doesn't shove it away. He wants to please her.

He adds, serious now, "You said you were afraid your father would figure it out."

"He's going to," she says, even before the words have fully left his mouth, as though she knew what he might say. Her eyes shimmer and ripple, a pool of fear that makes him want to steal her away, to put her somewhere safe, away from the man that puts that dry whisper of fear into her voice.

"Let him," he says. His hands close about her tiny waist, the muscles and curves shifting against the tips of his fingers.

She shakes her pale head, saying nothing, her hair rippling in black waves. They've been through this before.

"Come," she says. Turning, she catches his fingers in her own, pulls him silently from the circle of children and puppets, her bare feet moving without sound across the dirt. He follows, as a leaf follows the curve of the current, joyous and without restraint.

"Here," she says, finally, as they reach the edge of a stream he's never seen before. The light is late afternoon, and it turns the trees an apple green and the bark a buttery hue. "Red Cap does not know this tributary."

She rarely says her father's name, and the sound of it makes his flesh break out in goose bumps, small hills that dot his arms and legs like tussocks. He rubs his arms with his palms, brisk and quick, willing the skin back down. Her father is just a man, he thinks, like any other, although he knows this isn't entirely true.

"Come," she says. She steps in the shallow of the river's wide blue body, pushing her green dress from her shoulders, letting it fall into the water. He will never get used to the sight of her body, never wants to get used to it, the way her skin flows over her bones, the strong legs, the wide curves of her hips, the tiny breasts with nipples like pink pebbles.

He steps forward, joins her in the shallow water, shivering through the cold and stones.

"I could eat you up, swim in you forever," he says.

"Don't," she says. "Don't tell me. Just…please…"

She takes his hand, slides it between the cleft of her legs. He curls his fingers so that they dip between the folds of skin, begin a slow sink into her wetness. She is slippery as tiny fishes through his fingers. Pulling him down, she is strong and swift and she cushions his body against the rush of water and the hard edges of stone. It takes nothing to make him as hard; he's been that way since he first saw her in the market, and now he enters her, stone above her, stone below. The water washes over them both as their bodies surge and retreat.

She says his name, over and over, whispered so low he can't hear her, only feel the movement of her mouth against his, only know it's his name by the shape of her lips. His fingers are caught in the tangled net of her hair and he leaves them there, tightens the weave.

Coming, he can't tell what's him and what's her and what's water, except by the heat of it. He gushes hot into all of this cool, and she is biting his lip, hard, so hard that he ducks his head and the water comes roaring over him. He cannot breathe, but he keeps his mouth against hers until she lets go and then he raises his head with a great gasp.

"You must not go to the market again," she says, after. He is on the bank and she is sliding her dress back up over her shoulders. "It's not safe."

"I am not afraid." He isn't. There is a pounding in his heart, and in the sides of his neck, but it is not fear, something else entirely.

He thinks of how he will win her from her father. He will go to him and prove that he is everything a waterman could want for his daughter. He will get her father's permission and then she will be his, they will be theirs.

"That," she says, and she lays a palm against his face. Her skin is cool and it makes him shiver. "...is exactly why it is not safe."

After a beat she says, "Promise."

He does, but he doesn't mean it. Not this time.

* * *

When he is sleeping, curled on the green bank in a place where he could not possibly be found, she leaves him and returns to the market, a higher watermark staining the hem of her dress a darker green. There is something in her face that closes, draws into itself like a snail as she walks among the stalls.

She bargains for butter. Slides it between hands like a fish between stones. When her hands are full, she pulls the hem of her damp skirt up to carry the bars of golden cream.

There are so many things she will not do. She will not return to him, sleeping, even though her body already aches for his entry, and for the way he watches her as though he would drink her up. She will not tell him that her father is dead, has been dead for a hundred years. She will not give him up, like she's given up all of the rest who've come before him, handed them over to be borne again, blue and still, into the bosom of the sea. She will not.

She weeps as she walks, salting the butter.

Somewhere deep in a riverbed of rock and shale, her husband sleeps a hundred years in one day. When he wakes, it will storm, fast and furious, the clouds letting loose their water until they are dry as bone.

After, the moon will rise, cupping itself in the dark clear sky, and her husband will don his red cap and sit on the banks of the river, in the place where it is still and deep and makes no sound. She will join him in her red stockings, spinning a vest for him of skin and hair. They will speak of things that married couples speak of. Or they will not talk and will be silent.

He will play his pipe made of a cream-and-crimson conch shell. She will sing, a song of yearning and lullaby. The men will come, drawn by his tune or her voice or the wild promise of the river's dark depths, and she will crush her spinning needle in her palm and keep her breath held in her chest, afraid it will be his face she sees.

Only after, when it is not his face but someone else's, shining up from beneath the surface of the water, bloated and pale as a buried moon, will she remember to breathe again. And she will think, as she always does of late, how there are many ways to drown.

MIND YOUR PEAS AND Qs

Allison Wonderland

You've all heard of sleeping your way to the top, but I'll bet you've never heard of sleeping your way to the bottom.

According to the guidelines outlined in *The Handbook for the Highborn,* Revised Edition, proof of princehood is determined by a man's ability to feel a pea wedged beneath a stack of twenty mattresses. Old-school rules stipulate that a man must be able to detect the pea through the pile in order to qualify as The Real Deal. If he fails the test, he is classified as A Phony Baloney and, as a courtesy to the perturbed princess, is kicked out of the palace on his keister.

The revised edition of the handbook contains an extra requirement, a bonus to princesses but an onus to many princes. As outlined in the addendum, men must now demonstrate their authenticity through a test of endurance.

This is accomplished by the fine art of fornication. Every night, one mattress will be removed from the heap, diminishing the distance between the prince and the pea. If the man is a genuine prince, he will be able to feel the pea more acutely, as though he is lying atop—and grinding against—a bowling ball. At no time will the princess assume a horizontal position, as it is the man's authenticity that is in question, not hers. Men who pass the test, who prove that they are honest-to-goodness princes, will be granted permission to date the princess.

Since its publication three months ago, *The Handbook for the Highborn,* Revised Edition, has princesses all over the kingdom trembling in delight and their parents trembling in fright.

The royal rumpus room is abuzz with the chatter of tongues and the clatter of teacups. I have come upon a heated game of canasta. Hardly the right time for a serious discussion, but then, isn't the right time *always* the wrong time? I scan the room in search of my parents, who are somewhere among the huddled masses. They must be wearing civilian clothes, I realize, because I'm having difficulty locating them. My parents have a bit of a superiority complex, you see, and I hardly recognize them without their customary capes and crowns. At last, I spot them at a card table in the center of the room. I approach with caution.

"Hello, Mother. Hello, Father."

My parents peer at me over the tops of their playing cards. Their eyes are narrowed like coin slots and their lips are puckered like change purses. "Yes?" they query in unison, rising to their feet.

I gulp, forcing my heart down my throat and back into my chest. "There's something I'd like to discuss with you," I request.

Father sets his cards onto the table. A slick smile graces his face. "Now, sweet pea, we've been over this a thousand times," he says, as I escort my parents to a corner of the room.

"But, Father, I'm nearly thirty. Don't you think I'm old

enough to start dating?" (Screwing I've been doing for years now, but dating is a different story entirely.)

Mother shakes her head, her golden curls swishing from side to side. "We most certainly do not. Thirty is much too young. Give it another ten or fifteen years. Then we'll talk."

I thrust my lip forward in a pout. "But you promised."

Father straightens his slouch, trying to intimidate me with good posture. "Promised what?"

"That I could start dating."

"*We* said that?" Mother scoffs. "*We* agreed to such nonsense? You must have caught us on an off day."

"But that's unfair," I protest. "That's unreasonable. That's unethical. That's—"

"Oh, all right, all right," Mother interjects, her nerves beginning to unravel. "Clearly you're not going to let up until we give in, so…you win. We'll allow you to date."

"Oh, phooey!" Father grouses, a veritable grouch.

"If," Mother continues, conditioned to impose conditions, "we find someone suitable. Not only must the man you date be a prince; he must also be a prince of a man."

"Well, of course," I agree. "I wouldn't go out with just any crumb who comes along. I want to date someone I have a lot in common with—two peas in a pod, as the saying goes. Someone who is highly intelligent—he should be well bred and well read. And of course he must be a full-blooded blue blood. After all, only a purebred prince with a royal pedigree is good enough for me."

Father chuckles, his eyes crinkling, his pupils twinkling. "Do you want to date a person, sweet pea, or a poodle?"

"What a splendid idea!" Mother chirps. "Instead of a date, we'll get you a dog!"

* * *

For six months, Mother, Father, and I pore over applications from nearly every eligible bachelor in the kingdom. My parents place an announcement (not an advertisement, they insist) in *The Daily Dignitary*, alerting their subjects to the availability and desirability of their little princess.

The selection process has been a royal pain. Of the 800 men who applied, 799 failed to pass muster. Take Possible Prince Number 73, for example, who cited tonsil hockey as his favorite sport and listed fortune-telling and making shadow puppets as his hobbies and interests. Then there was Possible Prince Number 127, who prides himself on being a very experienced husband, having been married eight times. This came as no surprise when we reached the Heroes and Heroines section of the application, under which the candidate had named Elizabeth Taylor.

Possible Prince Number 361 was even less appealing, describing himself as a monarch-in-the-making and divulging his dream of sitting on a throne. I'm afraid the only throne he'll ever have the privilege of sitting on is the one in the lavatory.

My favorite applicant, however, has to be Possible Prince Number 507, who wrote extensively about the length of his libido, boasting that his cock was comparable in size to a yard-stick. Upon taking his measurements, I discovered that the information contained in his application was not only an exaggeration, it was a complete fabrication. I assure you that the only way he would ever be considered well hung is if he were swinging from the gallows.

And now we come to Possible Prince Number 712, Nolan, the only candidate whose application did not meet its demise in the paper shredder. His responses to our questions were clear, concise and creative. Under General Information, he wrote (in legible print, I might add):

I should probably tell you that I'm a vegetarian. This doesn't mean that I'm a picky eater, though. I'll eat anything—as long as it doesn't baa, moo, oink, quack, gobble, or cluck. I also have a passion for philosophy. I like to ponder all of life's mysteries. For instance, who put the bop in the bop-shoo-bop-shoo-bop? Who put the ram in the rama-lama-ding-dong?

Impressed, we scheduled an interview. For two weeks, I have been waiting, anticipating our meeting. But I've also been feeling apprehensive. Candidates were not required to submit a photograph with their application, so I have no idea what Nolan looks like. I suppose his appearance, stud or dud, is relatively unimportant, but I'm really hoping for a hunk.

I get the hunk I'm hoping for. I feel relieved, as this could easily have turned out to be a case of be-careful-what-you-wish-for. Nolan is handsome, with royal blue eyes, a body like an action figure and a smile that stretches from ear to ear.

After the interview, I escort Possible Prince Number 712 to the guest room. "Tell me about your family," I request, as we begin to disrobe. "Aside from your lineage."

Nolan removes his blazer. "Well, Dad is an aviator and martial arts instructor," he says, loosening his tie. "Mom is an interior decorator and former beauty queen who once competed against Delta Burke."

I set my blouse and skirt onto a chair. "Did she win?" I ask, reaching for the belt wound around his trousers.

His shirt finds its way to the floor. "I'm not at liberty to say," he replies. I think he winks, too, but I can't be certain, as my attention is presently directed to the ripples and stripes carved into his chest.

It isn't long before Nolan is completely unbuttoned and unbuckled. I scrutinize his lower half. Even flaccid, his phallus is inspiring, with its plump head and solid shaft, curved like a velvet rope.

We approach the ladder erected beside the piled-high pyramid. Dismissing his protests of ladies first, I insist that Nolan go ahead of me. I'm not being courteous; I'm being libidinous. While he ascends the ladder, I perform an assessment, noting the way his ass arches as he moves, the way his flesh flexes as he climbs.

When we reach the top mattress, I instruct him to lie in a recumbent position. Nolan complies, without hesitation, without reservation. He whimpers when his back connects with the mattress, but the pain does little to curb his burgeoning arousal. I watch as his cock grows hard and hardy, until it resembles the marble pillars in the vestibule.

I straddle his lips. His mouth roams from my curls to my clit to my cunt.

I straddle his hips. His hands roam from my neck to my nipples to my navel.

Groans clamber along my larynx. Goose bumps strain against my flesh. I pick up speed quickly, slamming my pelvis against his, cramming his cock deeper into my cunt.

"Please be gentle," he implores, and I grant his request, observing the distortions and contortions of his face, the agony of his ecstasy.

When we are through, we climb down from the tower. I permit Nolan to sleep on a regular mattress in a regular bed, while I retire to my bedroom. I'm an old-fashioned girl and have no intentions of sleeping with a man until I'm married.

The test continues for the next three weeks. Each night, one more mattress is removed, bringing Nolan closer and closer to the source of his suffering. He continues to perform with vigor, though his incessant sniveling tempers his enthusiasm.

The Handbook for the Highborn, Revised Edition, states that a princess has complete authority in ascertaining a prince's stamina. This means that a princess may reward a prince who tries to grin and bear it, or fault a prince who chooses to suffer in silence. I favor the latter, as I don't consider a man who opts to "take it like a man" much of a man at all.

By the time he has slept his way to the bottom, Nolan is black and blue and red all over. I inform him, cheerful yet contrite, that he has passed the test, and bestow upon him the coveted title of The Real Deal.

"Let me guess," he jests, his sense of humor the only part of him that's still intact. "You put a pea under the mattresses?"

I smile.

"Perhaps I will find a carrot under the sink?"

I shrug.

"Princess, now that I've passed the test, am I entitled to a little rest and relaxation?" he entreats, inspecting his bruises.

"Yes," I agree. "And you know what else you're entitled to?"

"A massage?"

I knead the knots near his spine. "Yes, and something else, too."

"What else is there?"

I kiss the plump plum bruise invading his left shoulder. "Peas and quiet."

IN THE DARK WOODS

Kristina Wright

Anthony's wife worships at Sacred Heart Catholic Church, two blocks from my condo in the city. They drive in from the suburbs because Sacred Heart is the only Catholic church in the area that still observes Latin mass. Anthony's wife prefers the old-fashioned church services of her childhood to the contemporary version offered in the bland suburban church near their stylish five-bedroom, three-bathroom home. Each Sunday, Anthony dutifully drives his wife and their two little girls to church and drops them off at the curb in front of that imposing stone building. Then he drives a block to the coffee shop where he will get the Sunday *Times* and an extrahot double latte, killing time while his family attends services (and prays for his soul, presumably).

Or, he used to. That was before me.

We met at the Colley Café one particularly chilly autumn Sunday morning. I was nursing a nasty tequila hangover and sipping a heaven-sent chai latte when he strolled in, wearing gray chinos and a black sweater, looking like the suburban dad he is. I didn't take much notice of him as he purchased his newspaper and latte and settled into the red overstuffed chair catty-corner to mine. He was a hairy Italian guy with a well-fed belly and an expensive gold watch on his wrist to match the gold band on his ring finger: most definitely not my type.

Our eyes met over the top of his paper and he arched one thick, dark eyebrow at me as if I had said something of which he disapproved. He stared a fraction of an instant too long to be polite. My pickup radar went off as I recognized the glimmer of interest in those dark, unreadable eyes. Even though I looked like Technicolor death in my pink and red flannel pajama pants and purple Stockley Gardens Art Festival sweatshirt, my dirty blonde hair twisted in a knot on top of my head, the Italian guy thought I was hot. That spark of desire in his eyes felt like a physical touch and left me with a surprising ache between my thighs.

We started talking and discovered we had absolutely nothing in common. He is a financial advisor with a wife and two kids, a hefty mortgage and a time-share in Orlando. I'm a happily single artist who pays the bills waiting tables and teaching middle-aged women how to find their inner goddess through yoga and belly dancing. Anthony is only five years older than me, but he lives in a different world—a world of two-week vacations and mini-vans with screaming children and rigid rules of right and wrong. That first Sunday, Anthony told me he liked my laugh and my ladybug pajama pants. I liked his big, strong-looking hands and the way his dark eyes never wavered from mine when I told him I hadn't had sex in nearly two months.

Three Sundays later we gave up on small talk and gave in to temptation. On the pretense that Anthony wanted to see some of my art, we walked the short distance from the coffee shop to my building. That familiar walk felt like the walk of shame before the deed is done. I was getting ready to take a married man to my bed and fuck him. I'm no angel—I've been with my share of guys who were supposedly already in a relationship, but though I had toyed with the committed and the affianced, Anthony was my first married hookup. What surprised me was not the guilt, but the lack of it. I didn't give it a thought. The only thing I could thing about was fucking him, feeling those big hands on my body and his cock—hopefully as big as his hands—moving inside me.

I was painfully aware of Anthony behind me, staring at my ass, as we climbed the stairs to the third floor of the brownstone where I lived. I kept waiting for him to touch me—wanting him to—but it never came. My hand trembled, jangling my keys loudly, as I let us into my condo and his deep laugh at my awkwardness eased my nerves. It felt as if we were moving in slow motion as we crossed the threshold and a tingle of rest-less anticipation danced along my rigid spine. Then he laid his big, warm hand across the back of my neck as the door closed behind us and my sigh was almost a moan.

I led him directly to the bedroom, feeling no need to play coy at this point. We both knew why we were here—and it wasn't so Anthony could look at my watercolors and oils. Sunlight streamed through the drafty, hundred-year-old windows, illu-minating the white sheets on my rumpled, unmade bed. For a fleeting moment, my thoughts went to his dutiful wife sitting in the church a few blocks away, sunlight streaming in through stained glass windows. The sun shone on both of us that day, the virtuous woman and the whore. My twinge of guilt fled before it could take hold when Anthony gently turned me toward him. His hands were warm and steady, soothing.

He cradled my face in those large hands and placed the

sweetest, most chaste kiss on my lips as we stood beside my bed. I knew this was the point of no return. He was giving me the option to walk away. I could say no. I could be virtuous, too. Instead, I whimpered one word against his soft lips. "More."

He gave it to me. He gave it all to me that first Sunday afternoon on my unmade bed. While his wife knelt in prayer two blocks away, he knelt between my thighs, thick and rigid, his cock all I had prayed for.

When he entered me that very first time, I cried out, over and over again, "Oh, god!"

For six months, with the exceptions of Christmas and Easter, when even bad Catholics make an appearance in church, Anthony has worshipped my body every Sunday as if it is the only cathedral he will ever need to enter. When I let myself think about it, which isn't often, I feel the sharp edge of guilt knocking against the ache of desire. I push it aside because I want him so bad he makes me ache—and because being with him has opened up something inside me, unleashing a frenzy of creativity I've never experienced before.

I spend the nights between our meetings painting. I don't go out with friends anymore; I don't want to. I want to fuck Anthony—and if I can't satisfy that desire, I want to be alone and paint. Canvases are lined against the walls and perched on windowsills. The longer I am with him, the more...feral, for lack of a better word, my art has become. My art is darker, wilder, almost frightening. And in some of my work, I find myself painting Anthony. But not the Anthony I know, or at least not the suburban dad he appears to be. No, the creature in my paintings is the man who brings out this wildness in me in bed and in my art. The guilt of being with him never goes away completely, but it seems a small sacrifice for what Anthony gives me in return.

Anthony has no such guilt about being with me. I ask him, but the answer is always the same.

"She has her faith and I have mine," he tells me, using his long fingers to part my plump labia. He opens me to his heavy-lidded gaze, hovering over me like a dark devil while his cock lies thick and hard against his thigh.

I moan, writhing in anticipation as I clutch the brass headboard. "What is your faith?"

"This," he says, slowly pushing a thick finger inside of my wetness. "Desire is the closest we get to heaven in this life. Passion is sacred."

I am intrigued even while I'm aroused. He slides a second finger in me and I nearly come off the bed. He knows how to touch me, this middle-aged, middle-class suburban husband and father. He knows what I need and he gives it to me like a gift.

"That sounds like sacrilege," I gasp.

His laugh is fiendish as his fingers coax me into incoherence, gliding over the engorged bump of my G-spot like it was a worry stone. "I don't believe anything is sacred," he says. "But I believe in fucking you."

I don't know what I believe in, but at that moment it doesn't seem to matter. All I know is his fingers are moving inside of me, stroking me in a way I've never experienced. An image of Michelangelo's *The Creation of Adam* flits through my fevered brain—God reaching down to touch Adam, their fingers not quite touching. Anthony's fingers inside of me are like the fingers of God, creating me from the inside out. Conjuring my soul into existence from the sheer will of his dark desire, making me in his image. And then making me come.

He slides his fingers wet with my arousal into my mouth as he pushes his cock into me, thick and ready, an instrument of my torture and ultimate release. I moan around his fingers, tasting myself, tasting what he has done to me. His heavy body above me, thrusting deep inside me, no longer seems divine. He fucks me into oblivion like an incubus intent on possessing me body and soul. I wrap my legs around his broad back and give myself over to this knowing demon who makes me scream and beg.

"Fuck me," I moan desperately into his ear. "Oh, god, fuck me hard!"

He pulls back, his expression feral. "God has nothing to do with it," he says in a voice that is little more than a guttural rasp. Then he comes, the demon inside him appeased for now.

Later, when it is time to leave, he notices my newest painting. "I like this. It has your passion. Angel and demon, huh?"

I'm not sure what he means; my brain is fuzzy from the rush of endorphins. I look at the painting as if for the first time, seeing it through his eyes. A nude couple writhes on a forest bed of green and brown foliage while countless bloodshot eyes watch them from the gray shadows. Watch them and condemn them. The lovers are Anthony and me, though I hadn't intended it that way. But the woman is pale and blonde like me and the man...well, he's hardly a man at all. His body is huge, hairy, ruddy. He almost blends into the forest background. His ears sweep up into points and on top of his curly dark head are two small horns.

"Angel and demon," I whisper as I close the door behind him. What is this demon doing to me? Do I even care?

Anthony is not the best lover I've ever had, but he is the most intense. I am languid and sore after he leaves me to pick up the family at Sacred Heart. I feel stoned and the world is a beautiful, hazy image through my orgasm-colored glasses. I have never felt this way with another man, have never woken the morning after sex feeling so well used that I ache. I cherish every love bite he leaves on my breasts and neck; I press obsessively at the bruises left by his big hands digging into my hips, thighs and ass, causing myself a pain that is but a fleeting memory of the pain I desire. If not for these marks, I wouldn't believe Anthony existed outside of my paintings.

Our relationship, if you can call it that, only exists on Sunday. Our time is short—two or three hours at the most—and it never feels like enough. This is the only time he has to himself, he tells me. Work and family suck up the rest of his time. Once or twice a week he calls me, but I never answer. I wait for him to leave a message and then I listen to it, again and again, like a favorite song. He whispers dirty things in his messages, promises of how he will fuck me when we are together again, and how he will make me beg for more. I imagine him at home, the wife making dinner, the children playing in the yard and him, pacing the length of his study like a caged animal, thinking about how he will fuck me the next time. I paint with these images in my head, butting up against the images of the perverse things we have done on my white sheets.

The Sunday after Easter, my cunt is wet before I even hear him coming up the stairs. It's been two weeks and I'm hungry for his body. My arms and neck ache from hours of painting, but even painting cannot satisfy this deep ache inside me. I *need* him. I'm standing in the doorway in nothing but a white T-shirt when he makes it to the landing. There are no preliminaries, no catching up on what each of us has been doing in the two weeks since we were last together. Our need for each other is too strong.

He grabs me in his arms and kisses me hard, nothing soft or gentle about him. I have the fleeting feeling I should be afraid, but I'm not. I am already high, my pulse throbbing. I melt against him, molding my body to his, as he squeezes my ass and presses his erection against me. I moan into his mouth, rubbing my bare pussy over the crotch of his pants. I don't care if I get him wet, I want to mark him the way he marks me every time we are together.

"I'm going to fuck you so hard," he promises as I wrap my legs around his waist.

I gasp, "Yes, please."

He carries me like that to the bedroom and tosses me on the bed. He strips while I watch and his naked, bearlike body makes me squirm on the bed. A dense forest of black hair fans across his broad chest and tapers down his stomach, his cock jutting from a tangle of black curls. He looks more like my fantasy creatures than ever before. He looks like the demon in the woods. I moan, slipping from the bed to my knees in front of him.

Wrapping my hair around his hand, he looks into my eyes. "You look like an angel."

I imagine myself as he sees me: pale, blonde and still wearing a white T-shirt. In contrast, his skin seems darker than it is because of all that black hair. His deep brown eyes are wild with an almost violent lust.

"You look like the devil himself," I whisper.

He laughs harshly. "No, I'm just one of the lesser demons."

I lick the length of his erection, from tip to root. His cock jerks against my tongue, coming alive beneath my touch. I take the head between my lips without using my hands as he guides me up and down by my hair.

I'm hot, so fucking hot, as if just being in his presence raises my body temperature several degrees. As I suck him, I strip off my T-shirt, releasing him from my mouth only long enough to slip the shirt over my head. My body is already slick with sweat, my cunt is dripping and I'm drooling around his cock. I slip him from my mouth and nestle his erection between my damp breasts. This makes him catch his breath, as if I have caught him by surprise. I look up and smile, not feeling the least bit angelic. If not for our civilized surroundings, I could almost believe we were the forest lovers from my painting.

I cup my breasts in my hands and slide up and down, letting his cock glide in the damp valley between them. He groans in appreciation, his hand tightening in my hair, pulling my head back so that my neck arches. I stare into his eyes and whimper, the hair-pulling triggering a visceral submissive response. I want to please him—I *need* to please him—and I squeeze my breasts around his cock and quicken my pace, anticipating his orgasm.

He jerks away from me suddenly. "What the hell?"

I look where he is holding his cock, see the streak of blood up the shaft. "Oh, god, I'm sorry," I say, fumbling with my necklace.

He notices it then, the small silver cross on a chain around my neck.

"Where did that come from?"

I am oddly embarrassed, as if I've been caught looking at porn. "My mother gave it to me for Easter."

"Damn thing is sharp," he says gruffly, his erection flagging.

I feel bad but can't help but giggle. "Ironic, huh?"

The lust is back in his eyes and he reaches for me. I think he's going to rip the chain from around my neck, but he only turns it so the cross hangs down my back. Then he nestles his semi-hard cock between my breasts. Staring into my eyes, he cups my breasts and moves against me, rubbing his thumbs across my nipples. His erection returns, hot and hard as before, and I grip his thighs as he rubs against my body. He begins tugging at my nipples, and the sensation goes right to my clit. I ache for him to fuck me, but I want this, too. I love the feel of his hard cock against my damp flesh as I kneel before him.

His strokes become faster as he squeezes my tits around his shaft. He is like a wild thing, humping my chest with no thought for my pleasure. I thrill at the look in his eyes and gasp when I feel the first hot spurt splatter against the swell of my breasts. Sucking my bottom lip between my teeth, I taste the ocean, salty musk. Whether it's my sweat or his semen, I don't know, maybe both. The taste is intoxicating and I suck harder until I taste blood. All the while he is thrusting against me, satisfying himself.

He slumps down on the edge of the bed and his eyes have lost that dark predatory look. I remain kneeling, heat radiating through my body. There is still a hum of anticipation dancing along the surface of my damp skin. I know my pleasure is to come, and I savor that feeling like a piece of hard candy melting on the back of my tongue. I rest my head against his hairy thigh, biding my time, pressing my hips together as I begin to writhe with my own rising desire.

"Would your god approve?" He pulls me up beside him and his fingers find my swollen clit.

It is hard to think when he's touching me like this. I shake my head, tendrils of hair clinging to my face. "I don't know. I don't care."

In that moment, with his thumb stroking my clit and his fingers pushing inside me, opening me up, I really *don't* care. I only care about this feeling—an ache like a hot stone at the core of my being—a need that only he can quench with his fingers, his mouth and his cock. In that moment, he is my dark muse and the only thing in the world I need—and I do *need*. He mounts me then—and that is the only word that describes the way he presses my knees back toward my shoulders and pushes his newly hard cock into me—and fucks me until I scream.

His words come back to me after he has gone. *My god.* He

has never asked me about my religious beliefs, though I have questioned his. *My god.*

Would my god approve?

It's the following Sunday morning and I sit in my bedroom, sunlight streaming in the window. I finger the cross around my neck like a touchstone, aching like an addict in need of a fix. Anthony is already twenty minutes late, and I am not sure he will come today. I look at my newest painting. It's only half finished, but it will be an orgy of bodies on a bed of red satin. At the center of all the decadence is a satyr who looks like Anthony. I smile.

Fleetingly, I wonder if he is sitting in a pew at Sacred Heart next to his wife and children, worshipping a god he doesn't believe in. If he never comes back, I wonder if he will think of me as I'm sure to think of him. Will he remember me as his angel or his whore? How will I remember him? A sharp pain pierces my breastbone: fear of losing what only Anthony gives me. I feel as if I'm drowning. Or dying. What will happen to me if he doesn't come back? What will happen to my art?

I hear heavy footfalls on the stairs and my pulse accelerates. I'll save the questions for another day because *he* is here, at last. Anthony.

My dark-haired devil. My demon muse. *My god.*

GILDI AND THE UNWIELDY, INEFFECTUAL COMMITTEE OF BEARS

Jeremy Edwards

This "spring fling" was the kind of gig that Gildi wouldn't be doing much longer. Sure, these campus festivals were good, easy money—especially for a headlining act—but it was simply getting too hard for her manager to work them into the touring schedule without sacrificing more important opportunities. "We can't start turning down late-night TV appearances to entertain a bunch of drunken college kids," Gary had told her with typical bluntness.

Gildi *liked* college kids—even drunken ones, up to a point. It hadn't been so long ago that she'd been a part of this world, at a campus a thousand miles away...messing around as a song-writer while she earned a degree in anthropology. She could easily remember a time, still in the relatively recent past, when the only gigs under her belt were school parties.

Then there were the literally under-her-belt performances—definitely a highlight of her college days and nights. Her lifestyle nowadays meant that most of the sex happened with musicians, with record-company staffers, with producers and journalists and other people she crossed paths with in the course of pop-music business. But checking out college guys always made Gildi happy. They were nice, fresh fodder for the part of her mental machinery dedicated to self-pleasuring—machinery whose corner of her mind Gildi visited as often as possible. So when Gary had explained that "the student association dude can put the band up in some kind of co-op, if we want to save on a hotel," Gildi had been more than okay with that. The more time she spent around dorm men—even if she didn't touch them—the better stocked her masturbation cupboard would be.

The cooperative dormitory had an official name that Gildi had already forgotten, but she was aware that it was more casually known as the Grizzly Commune, in deference to the university mascot. In fact, she had learned from the S.A. dude, residents of the co-op proudly called themselves "grizzlies," in a sort of countercultural twist on jock and frat culture that dated to the co-op's origins in the sixties.

The sound check was finished, but her bandmates had elected to stick around and watch the other acts. Gildi had decided instead to make her way to the co-op, telling her colleagues that she needed a nap—though what she really needed was some private time with her fingers between her legs. What with one thing and another, Gildi hadn't gotten off in days—not even with herself—and at this point, with professional obligations dormant until showtime, her libidinous itch was her top priority. As she walked toward her temporary home, responding to every appealing guy with a tangible flutter in her crotch, her over-riding thought was that she couldn't wait to yank her cutoffs down and get started.

When she entered the century-old mansion that had been repurposed into Grizzly Commune, she was confronted with a hunky but spacey looking young man behind a reception desk. She stared at his focus-free blue eyes for a few moments, waiting in vain for him to look up from the graphic novel he was reading and greet her. She gathered she would have to take the initiative.

"Hi. I'm Gildi. I think I'm supposed to be staying here tonight."

"Yeah," said the spacer, still not making eye contact. It wasn't clear to Gildi whether "yeah" meant "Yes, indeed, I have your room ready," or "If you say so, lady," or "Ask me if I care," or "I'm not actually paying attention but will acknowledge that you're speaking to me," or none of the above.

Gildi hesitated, not sure how to move the dialogue, such as it was, forward. But then Spacer followed up.

"I'm just covering someone's break. But hang on a second, and I'll see if I can find the guest log."

Gildi and her traveling satchel hung on a second, while Spacer read a couple more pages.

At last, he got up. Gildi observed that he had a tight, cute ass—almost reluctantly, given that she'd taken a justified dislike to him. He rummaged through some items on a large wooden table, producing a ledger of sorts. He leaned forward, his back to Gildi, and took his time flipping through the log, seeming to find certain pages nearly as absorbing as his comic book. She had a lascivious vision of sneaking up behind the guy, goosing him and tickling the taut meat between his ribs.

"I don't see any visitor rooms reserved for today. Oh, hang on." He tossed the ledger back on the table. "That's last year's."

Watching Spacer's wiry butt amble around the foyer while his glazed eyes made a perfunctory scan of the territory, Gildi became conscious of just how slick and restless she was getting inside her panties.

"I have no clue where the log is. Can you wait half an hour until my buddy gets back?"

Sure, she'd wait for his buddy—though she knew it was going to mean half an hour of seeping juice into her thong. Perhaps the "buddy" would be another hunk—this one with better circuitry above the neck, it could be hoped—and a glimpse of him would then make her postponed self-loving session that much richer.

She took out her laptop, sat on the floor, and caught up on band business for twenty-nine minutes. At that point Spacer peeked at his watch, rose from his comic-book station, and left the foyer, going up the stairs without saying a word to Gildi. Presumably, he was counting on his buddy to return the next minute, and he figured his assistance—if one could call it that— was no longer required.

But no buddy—nobody at all—showed up the next minute, or during any of the ten minutes that followed that one. Finally a beautiful, cleft-chinned guy, with low-slung jeans and a forest of curly hair, entered the building. Was this the buddy? Gildi wondered. She could certainly work with that. If *she* were picking a buddy, this was the kind she'd pick.

"Hey," said the guy, "do you know if it came in?"

"Sorry?"

"The delivery. For the kitchen. I'm supposed to cook for tonight, but we're, like, out of everything. Weren't you at the food-supply subcommittee meeting?"

"No," said Gildi, snagging a hungry glance at the waistband of his jockey shorts, "I missed it." She continued politely, "Are you the one who's staffing the desk?"

"Yeah," Buddy replied. "Technically." And he, too, disappeared up the stairs, his long denim legs mesmerizing her as he receded.

Gildi toyed with the idea of pursuing these handsome griz-zlies up the stairs. What would Spacer do if she confronted him on the landing, threw her arms around him, and squeezed her warm breasts into his torso as hard as she could? What would Buddy say if she cornered him outside his room and reached daringly for his fly? She pressed her thighs together with relish but dismissed this impulsive train of thought.

A moment later, she heard a vehicle in the driveway, and the sounds of people clattering in through a side entrance to the house. She slipped her computer back in her bag, stood up—noticing how dramatically damp her panties were—and called out, "Hello!"

Three college men emerged from a hallway—a bulked-up athletic type in a tank top, shorts and sandals; a skinny, tattooed guy dressed in black; and an officious looking redhead, all glasses and freckles. Each one was kind of hot, Gildi decided, in his own way—from the jock's obvious brand of studliness to the hipster's sinuous quasi-androgyny to the nerd's round-faced version of "geek cute."

"Hey," said Black-Clothing Guy, "Aren't you Gildi?" He was evidently too cool to put much pizzazz into the question, but a hitch of his eyebrow conveyed that he was impressed.

"Yeah!" said Gildi with relief, extending a hand. "I've been waiting for someone to direct me to my room."

"Your room?" said Freckles and Glasses.

"Uh-huh," she said, addressing herself to what she presumed was an ally in Black-Clothing Guy. "I'm supposed to stay here tonight."

"That can't be right," said Athlete. "Maybe you're here *next* Saturday, the twenty-seventh?"

Gildi couldn't help rolling her eyes, but she spoke calmly. "The student association arranged it, because I'm performing at your Spring Fling. I think you're supposed to look in the guest log—assuming you can locate it."

Freckles and Glasses shook his head. "Nah, the log won't do any good if it was arranged through the S.A."

"Do we still have a VIP spreadsheet on the upstairs computer?" asked Black Clothing.

"The spreadsheet wouldn't reflect an S.A. booking, either," said Athlete. "They only use that for visiting lecturers—things the faculty liaison sets up."

"Besides," said Freckles, "that computer is in the shop."

"Maybe I should just get a hotel room," said Gildi. She was beginning to lose patience. Irritation quivered through her above the waist, while her libido continued to pulse below.

The guys ignored her. "Who's chairing the facilities subcommittee this month?" asked Black Clothing. Despite her annoyance, Gildi admired the sleek, kissable line of his neck.

"Jen," said Athlete. "But she's downstate this weekend, at a job fair."

Black Clothing reacknowledged Gildi at last. "I have Jen's cell number, though she's probably not taking calls while she's doing interviews. What time do you have to crash?"

I am in immediate need of a bed to masturbate on—before my clit burns a goddamn hole through my shorts. That was how she wanted to respond. But although she had a frank vocabulary, and two of her songs had earned "explicit lyrics" tags because she'd used the work *fuck*, this wasn't the type of thing she usually blurted out.

"To tell you the truth," she said untruthfully, "I could use a nap ASAP."

"Maybe she could borrow one of our rooms for a while," said Athlete.

"I don't know," said Freckles. "We should really clear it with the facilities subcom...or at least with the rules team."

"They're meeting Thursday," Black Clothing said helpfully to Gildi.

She revisited a thought she'd shoved aside earlier—the option of excusing herself to one of the co-op's bathrooms and jilling off on the toilet, on the floor, or even against the wall. But once again she resisted this alternative. After days of celibacy, she'd been looking forward to a proper, sensuous, *comfortable* pussy-pampering, and she didn't want to throw away the highly antici-pated quality time in favor of a cramped diddle.

"Screw it," said Athlete magnanimously, his appetizing muscles rippling under his tank top. "I'm gonna chance it. You can nap in my room," he said to Gildi. "Second floor, first door on the right. It's not locked."

She thanked him, took her satchel, and headed up the stairs toward release.

As she neared the landing, the taste of the scheduled orgasm already real to her, she heard someone switch the radio on downstairs.

...right here on your campus radio station. It's coming up on three, and...

When she let herself into Athlete's room, she was surprised to hear a voice—the campus DJ's voice that she'd just left behind. She noted that Athlete had a pair of hulking speakers mounted from his ceiling, and she deduced that they were wired so as to pipe in whatever the house system was playing.

She tossed her satchel on the floor, peeled back Athlete's comforter, and let her ass sink luxuriantly into his mattress. She closed her eyes in anticipatory rapture as she unsnapped her cutoffs and let her fingertips slither into her panties.

We continue now with our weeklong "Music of Broadway" festival...

Fuck! thought Gildi. She loved an enormous variety of music, but this was one genre she just couldn't do. Especially if they were going to play stuff like

...the title track from Rodgers and Hammerstein's Sound of Music.

As the all-too-familiar strains began, Gildi opened her eyes and pulled her hand out of her shorts. She might be the horniest gal on this sprawling campus, but there was no way she could get off to such noxious accompaniment.

She made a breakneck visual journey around the room, hoping to spot a stereo receiver or other control box—anything with an OFF switch or a volume knob. But there was nothing. The speakers, it seemed, were connected directly to the equipment on the ground floor. Short of yanking the wires out of them—and she was tempted—there was nothing she could do to can the unwelcome soundtrack.

She grabbed her bag and ran downstairs, where she found the three guys eating sandwiches in the kitchen.

"I'm sorry," said Gildi. "The radio...I can't, um, sleep."

Athlete shrugged. "I guess we could turn it off."

"But then we'll lose it down here!" said Freckles, petulantly. "I wanted to hear this."

I'm the one who's about to lose it, thought Gildi. Even as she suppressed the urge to scream at Freckles, she noticed the boy's adorable little frown. She wondered if he was a virgin.

"Okay," said Black Clothing, looking back and forth from Gildi to his friends. "You can use my room. I don't have any speakers up there. Third floor, second door on the left."

Gildi raced back up the stairs, and up the next flight, more excited than ever about what she had in store for herself. She flung open Black Clothing's door, closed it behind her, and dove onto his futon.

She rolled over and scooted backward, compressing the black-clad pillows and propping her shoulders against the wall. Spreading her legs wide, she relaxed, her gaze settling on a dresser across the room—where she was astonished to see another pair of eyes staring back at her.

Feline eyes.

"Oh, no, no, *no!*" said Gildi, out loud. "No!" she repeated, to no one in particular. "I will *not* masturbate in front of a cat."

The guys were still in the kitchen.

"I'm sorry," she said to Black Clothing, "but I didn't realize you had a cat. I'm, uh, allergic."

"Dude," said Athlete to his buddy, "can't you bring Björk down here?"

"Forget it," said Black Clothing. "Last time I did that, she hid behind the water heater, and it took me all freakin' day to get her out."

Freckles sighed. "Do you want to try my room?" He said it with a whine, as though he felt obliged to make the offer and resented her for it.

"Oh, god, yes," said Gildi emphatically, tuning out the whine and thinking only of her tingling pussy. Then, since her answer had resounded with what she assumed to be a puzzling level of enthusiasm, she clarified: "I'm...so very sleepy."

This was really it, Gildi verified, when she'd let herself into the last room down the right hall on the fourth floor. Radio free? Check. Animal free? Check. She dropped her bag and swung the door shut, then leapt onto the narrow dorm bed and wrapped her thighs around her ministering hand.

She was so horny, she didn't even bother to slide inside her pants right away—she just humped herself, for starters, against the heel of her hand, right through the stiff cotton of her shorts. The gratification was delicious—definitely worth the wait—and she moaned her appreciation of the self-delivered friction.

With leathery male buns and sweat-glistening pecs and thick college cocks swirling in her brain, Gildi wallowed on the borrowed bed. In her current state, it would have been asking too much of herself to keep a mental focus on a particular man or a particular scenario. Instead, she let the explicit fantasies come at her like a fast-motion montage—big hands wild on her breasts... beer-damp mouths clinging to her clit...needy shafts scraping in and out of her hot pussy from behind...her soft rear cheeks getting pinched and fondled and slapped into a squirmy heaven.

Now she unzipped her cutoffs—quickly wiggling them down and kicking them off—and gave herself the treat of direct contact: one delicate finger burrowing under her gusset, to plunge slowly in and out of her weeping hole. Her long-patient cunt sizzled with pleasure, intensely grateful for every stroke.

With her other hand, she started to tap, Morse-code style, on her swollen clit and with both hands on deck she danced to her own dreams. Time stood motionless while she kept her sex luxuriously nurtured yet still frantically yearning. She wanted to come, yes, but she also, paradoxically, wanted to pirouette on the rim forever. She was in paradise, desperate with arousal and yet fulfilled.

As she edged, one exquisite inch at a time, toward orgasm, the grizzlies began to appear onstage in her head. She imagined Spacer with his underwear at his ankles, his blue eyes wide while she handled his ass. There was Buddy, titillating her thighs with his fluffy curls while licking her pussy—giving her all the attention he'd neglected to provide in real life, and then some. Athlete hoisted her to fuck her in the air, her legs enclosing his rock-solid waist. Black-Clothing rubbed her nipples with long, sensitive fingers, while she deep-throated his cock. And Freckles...

Freckles burst through the door with a load of laundry.

"Crap!" He froze. "I forgot you were in here." He looked as if he might cry.

Gildi couldn't have stopped if she'd wanted to. On the contrary, the unexpected presence of her host—this zip-locked little sandwich bag of male hormones who had caught her gyrating with her finger up her snatch—was the final element that propelled her into the stratosphere. And so, unable and unwilling to do anything but come like a massive, slow-motion thunder crack, she just looked Freckles right in the glasses while she came like a massive, slow-motion thunder crack...trembling with utter ecstasy and flooding her hand, her thong and a small piece of the poor guy's bed with a warm gush of girl come.

Her mind went blank, and she watched the boy's freckles blur as her orgasm lasted and lasted. She writhed powerfully with each wave of the climax, kicking her legs and bouncing her sex-sensitized asscheeks on the bed.

She kept looking straight at Freckles, her eyes regaining their focus as the aftershocks tickled through her. She could see the ridge in his pants; apart from that, he still hadn't moved—not a muscle of his body, nor even a muscle of his face.

Finally, Gildi's body came to rest, and Freckles swallowed.

"Um...how's the room working out?" he said meekly.

Gildi smiled, sensing the beatific radiance of her own contentment. "It's just right," she said.

FROSTED GLASS

Aurelia T. Evans

When I was a little girl, my father told me not to look into the frosted windows on winter nights, for I would see the face of the Snow Queen, the witch who freezes hearts of young women for eternity with her piercing eyes. He was a good father, telling his warning stories that his father told his sisters in their youth. But like all little girls, with the curiosity of Eve deep in our beating hearts, I carried the candle to the window and peered into the glass. The wind was whistling outside and the warped glass was white with the star growth of ice. I brought the candle close to the patterns and marveled at the intricacy and beauty of the winter frost. The heat from the candle was not enough to melt it, although the crystals seemed to change as it came near. I could see the faint lines of my reflection as though it had been frozen into the glass: my blonde hair in braids, my upturned nose, my round cheeks, my bright blue eyes. All color was muted gray, but I could still see that it was myself in the icy impression.

The closer I looked, the more detail I could see in the glistening crocheted lace. Although the fire was burning and the room was comfortably warm, the cold seeped through the window and made my nose numb so close to the glass. As fascinating as the icy windows were, though, I was still young. I sighed when I saw nothing of the Snow Queen in the window. My impatient breath fogged the glass and as the moisture faded, it was then that I saw the image of the woman. I never once thought I was simply distorting the image of myself. The outline of the woman's face was faint but clearer and clearer the longer I stared. Although it was night outside, the Snow Queen seemed to glow with her own light. The hand holding the candle lowered and set it on the shelf—it was no longer needed—and I came closer to the window, to the soft blue glow in the frost, entranced. Her lips were moving, but I could not hear what she was saying, although there seemed to be whispers under the screaming of the wind.

I saw into the eyes of the Snow Queen. They were cold and empty, with the frigid beauty of blue ice, and a chill grasped my heart like fingers. I saw into the eyes of the Snow Queen when I was a little girl, yet I grew to love as fully and strongly, with the heat of my heart, as any woman.

My husband and I had a practical marriage, but it was not cold. Our marriage bed was warm and inviting after the vows and feasts. The warmth of Christian's body covered mine, filled me until I was burning and crying out, my golden hair splayed on the pillow. He was a keeper of a small textile shop, and his mother taught me to sew. We had an ordinary life marked with a few extraordinary moments: The day my father passed away. The picnic on the hottest of our summer days—we swam in the pond, and our clothes were filthy as we walked home, but we were so happy, and he removed my dress as though peeling off my skin to the heat of his gaze. The day his mother passed away.

The coal that jumped from the stove and set fire to our kitchen table. The fever that burned so hard I cut off my golden hair above my neck, sweat dripping down my face.

My heart was strong for ten years. It was after my winter fever, when I stood before the looking glass and my hands tried to touch the ghosts of my sheared hair, that Christian's heart froze. While I cried in bed, mourning something that I knew was vanity, he shattered the fogged and frosted mirror with his fist at my pain. I pulled pieces of bezel glass from his knuckles without a word, and I swept up the pieces when he left the room above the store to visit the bar. When he returned his face was stone sober, although his breath smelled of ale.

It should have been nothing. I could have lost my life, and my beautiful hair would return in time. Christian was not a material man—he used to be content with what little we had, and he loved me. He did, I know it in the depths of my soul. But all it took was one day, one bad day to sour everything. He was irrational, silent, cold. His eyes were glassy as he stared away from me, not seeing the woman he had been with for the last ten years.

I began to hear whispers in the store when the gossips thought that I could not hear, hisses of pity and judgment as they lamented my inability to keep my husband in the home rather than in the pubs, or in the beds of other young women. I cannot say that he strayed. I held him close when he came back to me at night, but I could not warm him. His heart wasn't mine, but it did not belong to another—it was just gone. He spoke, he ate, he talked, he sold, but there was nothing inside him that made him warm. And he never looked at me anymore. The scars from the shattered mirror faded into little white dots on his hand, but it was as though he had shattered me instead.

Then one night he did not come back to me. I shivered under

the covers, waiting for his body if not his love. But he never came home. I dressed in the light of a candle and wrapped his coat around me. The pub was still riotous when I arrived, shouldering my way through the throng of bodies and smelling sweat and alcohol and leather all around me. A hand pawed at my buttocks through the coat, or at least it tried. I continued on my mission, peering through the empty spaces, checking faces at the tables. I was not frantic or worried, but my face was flushed with intent. I did not find him until I stumbled up the stairs to the place where patrons went for a night or two to sleep off their hangovers and avoid the glaring eyes of their families. Very rarely were the rooms above the pub used as an inn—that establishment was on the other corner, a more respectable place.

I heard my husband before I saw him; a light, muffled slapping sound, and the breathy groans of a woman. I could smell her cheap perfume as I pushed open the door. They did not hear me, and if they did, they would not have stopped, so intent they were. Or she was, anyway, her head tossing with every thrust of his powerful hips, his cock entering into her in a rhythmic pace. Her expression was distorted in pleasure, but although Christian's erection was hard and strong, his face revealed nothing, his exclamations simply an indication of effort. Heartstrings tugged at my palms and tightened in my lungs as I watched him, her, her large breasts jiggling as she brought him into her, taking in a part of him that had not touched me since the fever.

Watching the soulless body of my husband was more chilling than any frosted window. I walked out the same way I came, the coat bundled around me. My footsteps against the stone were lost in the snowdrifts. I passed by the storefront: cold floors, cold sheets, cold bed, cold sleep. I did not think I could take so much coldness. The wind was screaming by the windows, but there was no fire inside to make the winter beautiful, no warmth to make it wonderful. Snow settled on my eyebrows, my eyelashes, my lips. It coated my short hair, and the frigid air wrapped around my now bare neck. From a distance, I must have appeared a shadow, a dark figure in the midst of the white snow and faint outlines of buildings.

I should not have stayed out in the storm. My mind swirled with thoughts of broken mirrors and ice crystals. I thought of lying down in a pool of shattered glass, waiting in pain for my husband to arrive. Maybe those shared shards of mirrored glass would remind him of his responsibility or harden my heart as much as his was hardened. I felt hollow, but only because I knew there was a part of me that could still accept that warmth and love—I did not think Christian even knew how empty he had become.

My feet brought me through the numbing cold all the way to the pond. I could barely see it through the darkness and the moonlit snowfall, but I remembered where I was. Circling and circling and circling the pond I went, going nowhere but taking all the time that I needed to get there, barreling through each eddy of snow. I knew each twist and turn of the pond's edge until I didn't.

When I was a little girl, my father told me never to wander far from home. Home could be a house, home could be a family, and home could be the town that had surrounded me since my birth. I could have stopped walking when the familiar surroundings suddenly became unfamiliar. Maybe the twisting of the landscape would have stopped, and I would have seen through the misty darkness to the few lit windows of the village. Maybe I would have found my way back to those stone-paved streets. But I didn't stop; I kept moving forward because there was nothing behind me worth returning to.

The frozen pond expanded into a frozen lake, until I could

not see its end on the horizon. The snow was packed more tightly around the ice than it had been at the pond, and my path led into an ice dwelling that was far more welcoming than the pub tried to be. I knew I was being called, every limb freezing underneath the inadequate clothing, because wherever I was, it was far colder than our worst winters.

She was waiting for me in the middle of the room, standing with bared skin on the iced lake. I could see the patterns of the ice crystals, giant stars on the surface. There were icicles coming from the ceiling like stalactites, and frozen snowdrifts that narrowed into sharp tips. In them I could see my reflection. If I looked closer into the glistening surfaces, I thought that I could see other reflections, eyes gazing through the patterns until their outlines became clear. The floor was a mirror, and I watched my feet meet their twins. I almost thought that I would fall through, so clear was the image of myself, colorless, expressionless, yet still with life in me. I could see it in the reflection of my eyes as they melted ice enough to see through the mirror. Under the ice, I could see human hearts that looked bright red and healthy. Perhaps they were even still beating. Perhaps one of them belonged to my husband.

I could have asked for her to return the heart to my husband, but the wish would have gone ungranted. The Snow Queen does not collect hearts unwillingly—shattered mirrors are hard to come by without a heart ready to rip from the chest, replaced with a chunk of ice surrounding stone. Once replaced, the body and the heart can never be as it was.

When I was a little girl, my father told me to never look into the Snow Queen's eyes, lest my heart freeze to the love of a man. My man's heart froze to me, and I looked into the Snow Queen's eyes. I was neither the first nor the last woman to stare into those icy blue eyes, almost like my own. Her fingers touched my pale cheek that could not even muster the blood for a blush.

She did not speak or could not speak. But her marble white lips parted, and I could hear her in my mind. She told me that I was welcome to stay, but all things that stayed must die. Nothing living could survive in a wasteland. Her fingertips on my cheek were frigid, and for a moment, I thought the blood froze in my veins. She did not need a cloak to stay warm because she had no warmth, nor need of it. Her flesh was soft but cold as snow, her eyes the only glimpse of anything like life, her blood a frozen river. There was only frosty breath when her mouth came close to mine, becoming moist with the heat beneath my skin.

"I don't want to die." They were the only words that had been spoken in this room for too long, and they made the walls vibrate and tremble. Icicles fell from the ceiling, and some shattered, sliding across the ice like skates or sleds.

She told me that I could have warmth and die, or I could freeze and cease to live. At first I did not understand, because they did not seem to be two choices. But then her lips touched mine lightly, and the blood beneath my lips froze, numb and stiff, yet I could still move them beneath hers. Ice cracked between the creases, and when I shivered, it was not because the cold was too great. I felt the cold seeping into me, inch by inch. A thin sheen spread over my skin, star patterns that radiated out. I blinked and heard a noise like nails on glass. My breath was still warm, and it felt like fire as her tongue slid along mine, drawing it into her mouth. For a moment, when my mouth was still warm, I stuck to her, my fingers trapped to her waist, her hands to my face, my tongue to her tongue. But the freeze deepened until it was as though ice was brushing ice, slick and wet and dry all at the same time.

My husband's coat fell from my shoulders, and the Snow Queen slowly ripped my gown from neck to navel. It joined the superfluous coat on the ice. My nipples were erect and hard, almost painful in the cold until there was no difference between myself and the air. I could actually feel when my heart stopped in my chest, as though there was a great stillness that would not be broken. But my heart was still there, not in her collection of shattered hearts beneath the ice. My lungs stilled, and I was unable to make a sound as the Snow Queen took a frigid nipple between her teeth, the pain as sharp as the cold.

My hips shifted as the warmth of pleasure between my legs swiftly froze, the moisture inside forming tiny icicles. The heat was gone, but the pleasure was not, caught in the moment when my flesh was engorged with blood. Her slippery tongue tangled in my hair there, tracing in a circle where the pleasure was greatest until I grew colder and colder, the freeze reaching my toes near where the Snow Queen knelt. I could barely move, but I pressed my hips to her face, my fingers gradually closing in the length of her white hair.

I thought of my husband, but the thought was brief, as his thought of me would be brief when he returned to the empty room and did not receive a warm breakfast in the morning. If he came home at all.

Something large and sharp pressed against my entrance, and I stretched for it as steadily as anything I or she could do. The long icicle inside me was bigger than my husband could hope to be, and every second felt that much longer than when I used to be warm, with my blood beating quickly in my veins. This was not a rush—this was a long, excruciatingly, exquisitely slow freeze. My mouth opened, but no sound came out—my lungs had frozen solid, and I could not find breath enough to speak. My moans stayed in my head, but the Snow Queen heard them, just as I could hear her soft exclamations. I was hers, one woman among many, a legion of Snow Queens in the vast frozen lake wasteland. No demons, no villains—just taking what was right-fully ours by divine law. The shattered mirrors, the frosted glass, the stone hearts, and the Snow Queens that neither spoke nor lived: walking ghosts, ethereal witches as ephemeral as breath on the window.

The icicle stretched me, its smooth ridges catching on the lip of my entrance and rubbing against a place in my body that had only been reached once and quite by accident. This time, though, the Snow Queen found it and used it until I felt like my flesh would shatter into a hundred jagged pieces like mirror shards. When she brought me to my climax, mouth still pressing to the hooded nub of flesh and icicle sliding in and out like I was liquid within, I heard the thousand cracks in my head, and I thought I saw someone in my mind's eye, a woman who had dropped her looking glass on the ground and pricked her finger on the ice of my gaze. The vision faded, but I held the stranger's heart in my hand, as hot as a burning coal.

The Snow Queen stood, guiding me to a place in the ice that opened for the new resident. Her bluish lips curved into a smile that was icily beautiful. I knew that it looked like mine. Pale skin against pale skin; blue eyes staring into blue eyes: it was like staring at my reflection in frosted glass.

GINGERBREAD MAN

Carol Hassler

Emily swayed as the sun filtering in through her half-shut kitchen blinds teased her awake. *Shit.* She had been sleepwalking again. David always told her she needed to tie herself down in bed. Often, grinning, he would do just that. *David.* She squeezed her eyes shut. Her head hurt. Everything, even her stupid sleepwalking, reminded her of him. "At least I didn't leave the apartment," she murmured, rolling her neck.

She opened her eyes and gasped, then staggered to catch herself on the edge of the table. Her hands, clutching the weathered maple of the large worktable, were covered in flakes of dried dough and her feet were unseen beneath the empty flour sacks that littered the floor like clouds. Emily clapped both hands to her mouth and stepped back hastily. The rational part of Emily slumped in the corner of her mind. *So this,* that tiny and coldly logical part mused, *is what it must mean to go mad with grief.*

The kitchen burned pinkly from the light filtering through the shades, flushing the sculpture on the table with an almost healthy glow. Stretched along the maple lay David—or rather, a life-size replica of him. Her hands, still pressed against her mouth, smelled strongly of spice: cinnamon, ginger, cloves. She thought she might vomit. Two months of her silent apartment after David died and she thought she had been getting better.

Emily flinched, remembering now the trip to the store, the piles of flour and sugar bags and spices swept from the rack into her cart. And the blessedly mindless act of kneading the dough, forming the legs, chest, head.

Oh, yes, she remembered now. Bright white lines of light had crawled along the floor, crept up the legs of the chairs and skirted the edge of the table by the time she lowered her hands. She stepped into the sunlight, so that her shadow loomed large against the kitchen wall. In her mind, rational Emily turned away politely. She ran her hand up the arm posed casually on the table, hand draped over the sculpture's stomach. The city hummed outside the window but the kitchen was close and private. *Nobody needs to know,* she thought, *that I've gone crazy.*

She bent her head until she hovered over the lips of the figure. The air, so heavily scented with cinnamon, clung to her hands and dusted her skin, blending her hand into the torso as she rested it lightly there. She closed her eyes, then pressed her lips against the model of her late husband, letting her mouth sink into the groove of his lips. She sighed at the familiarity. And then the dough began to settle under the pressure of her kiss and reality began to intrude. She flexed her fingers over the chest, ready to tear down the sculpture, break it into balls for the trash and then go have a good long cry in the shower.

The dough quivered. She would have dismissed it, so slight was the change, had she not still had her lips pressed against the sculpture. Startled, she drew back. The sculpture was changing somehow. The dough seemed to adjust, growing tighter in some places and flexing outward in others. As she watched, the soft impressions of features in the warm dough became hard lines of bone structure, then softly rounded muscle, then skin pocked with fine pores. The chest rose once, body arching upward at the waist in a sharp angle, and she lifted her hand in shock.

A long gasp rattled through the still room.

The body—there could be no other word for it—slammed into the table and instead of the gelatinous slap of dough, a hard thud resounded, as though from bone and hard muscle. The sculpture sat up.

It was insane: it was flour and spice and sugar. But she looked at the sandy lips and the chest moving in and out, and the eyes roving the kitchen to meet her own. Her heart broke and reformed at every detail. The thing, which was so like her husband, swung his legs off the table.

She backed against the counter, her stomach writhing as he stepped down. He stared intently at her. She felt nervous, confused, and strangely, deliriously happy. He wrapped his hands around her waist, stroking the thumb downward to rest on her hips. Slowly, he leaned forward, settling his weight against her, pinning her to the counter's edge.

And then she was enveloped in it. In him. He pressed his hips against her. Everything was hard, just as she had remembered it. Everything. He thrust against her belly, pinning her to the counter. He slid his hands from her waist, gently tickling up her torso to caress the sides of her breasts and throat through her soft nightgown. Carefully, he cradled her chin. He paused for just a moment and the smell of cloves and cinnamon was nearly overwhelming. His hands were warm and soft against her skin. Slowly he lowered his mouth, claiming her lips.

The kiss began gently. His lips teased at the corners and edges of her own. Then his tongue slid between her lips, deepening the kiss quickly. She only had a moment to marvel that he had a tongue at all before she lost herself. He tasted so strongly of spice it was nearly overwhelming; as she sucked on his tongue, the cinnamon came to the fore and made him taste like fire. That was different. Everything else, from the feel of his hair to the color of his skin—everything else was the same.

He moved to her neck, licking and sucking. Distractedly, she realized her nightgown was inching up, folding on top of his advancing hand as he slid it up her thigh. She moaned loudly and arched against him as he slipped up the gown to cradle her breast, then pulled off the flour-dusted garment. The countertop was cold where it pressed against her back, and she eagerly sank into the warm and yeasty musk bearing down on her. Somewhere in her distraction he had continued to grow more real. The lust that had enveloped her like a sudden summer storm calmed for a moment in wonder and she raised her hand to cup his face. David's familiar brown eyes stared deeply into her own and locks of his fine dark hair rolled across his forehead as he moved.

She wrapped her hand behind his head and pulled him in for a long, deep kiss. She gasped as his fingers slipped between her legs, rising onto her tiptoes as a sudden bolt of ecstasy shot through her. He cupped her buttocks, slipping his hand around to meet her inner thighs. Then, as he deftly turned her, she found herself pushed against the table and then sitting on its floured surface.

He kissed her once more, deeply, then began a trail of light licks and nips, pausing at her breast to suck her nipple before arriving at her delicate cleft. He licked her then and she shivered at his hard, probing tongue against her overly sensitive skin. She lowered her hands into his hair, caressing it, then clutching as his kisses grew deeper.

Teetering on the edge of her climax, Rational Emily gave one last protest—she was dreaming, or crazy. Then he raised his head and grinned, teeth white against his dark cinnamon skin. He grasped her hips and thrust inside her in one quick motion. For a long moment he paused, deeply buried, his body pressed against her, chest aligned with her own, eyes intent and tinged with something like worry. His lips parted as though to say something and, suddenly afraid, she grabbed him and pulled him in for a deep kiss, writhing along his penis, drawing him deeper within as her thighs parted farther.

He began to thrust then and she clutched him to her, noses nearly touching, sharing breaths, until she cried out, no longer able to hold in her voice against the silent lovemaking. The feel of him sliding against her brought her again to the edge and he lowered his head, sucking on her neck until she broke under him, the world disappearing. He pulsed against her quivering flesh before collapsing over her, palms flat against the table as his head burrowed into her shoulder. She was neatly pinned to the table and she raised her legs to encircle his waist.

"I love you," she said softly and stroked his torso gently, then his cheek. "If this is a dream, I hope it never ends." His eyes were soft after the intensity of their lovemaking, and he raised a hand to roll a lock of her hair between his fingers before tucking it behind her ear. She shivered again at the caress, then pressed her palms against his shoulders, pushing him back. Her brain seemed to work better with a little distance. "Am I still asleep?"

His lips formed the word No but nothing emerged from his mouth. His eyes widened as though in panic, mouth gaping.

"Shhh," she said needlessly, pressing a finger against his lips. "I must be asleep," she murmured as she nuzzled his sweet-smelling neck, enjoying the smell of sex strongly overlaid by cinnamon and ginger. "But I don't care." He trembled in her arms, then reached his own up to encircle her.

Some time later, she drew back. "Come on," she said, pushing him gently back and hopping back onto the floor. She ruefully held up her hands, still covered in dough, arms dusted in flour. "I need a shower." She grabbed his hand and dragged him after her.

He followed her, unprotesting and silent, down the short hallway and into the small bathroom. His hand was warm and dry and delightfully familiar. As long as she was mired in this odd dream, she would enjoy it. Emily smiled—she couldn't stop smiling. She turned on the water and held her hand under the stream, waiting for it to warm. Then she stepped inside, closing her eyes as the hot water flattened her hair and turned her powdered skin slick.

David, standing just beyond the doors, smiled slyly and moved to step past the curtain. In an instant, the delightful, glowing morning turned nightmarish. He had placed his hand under the stream to test its warmth when the skin on his hand began to bubble. The thick cinnamon scent that had overlaid the kitchen carried quickly through the steam. He snatched it back quickly, cradling his arm against his chest, hand curled in a claw of agony. He opened his mouth, face contorted, as though he was trying to scream.

Emily screamed. Half of his fingers on the hand were misshapen and one of them was simply gone—boiled away. "I'm still dreaming." She began to sob. "Still dreaming." She collapsed under the spray as he stared at her in shock. "You're still dreaming," she shrieked at herself. "Wake up," she sobbed. "Wake up." Again, she met his eyes. "Get out." She whimpered as she curled into a tight ball against the smooth bathtub. "Get out."

She shivered in the hot shower, huddled half under the spray. David stumbled back, hand held before him, then ran from the room. Minutes later she heard, beneath the pounding water, the front door slam.

She stayed under the shower for a moment more, then turned it off, deliberately slowly. Carefully, she raised herself and stepped out, wrapping a towel around her torso and tucking it under her folded arms.

The light in the bathroom shone with offensive cheer and she flipped off the switch, edging out the door. The apartment was utterly quiet. She walked to the bedroom. David's dresser drawers were pulled out and hung pathetically from the dresser body, clothes spilling from the edges.

She sat on the bed, numbly noting how her body trembled. She let the silence roll in and surround her. Beyond the ever-present hum of the street below, there was nothing and nothingness. She pinched her thigh, hard.

This didn't feel like a dream or even a nightmare. The quiet reality she had been living in for the past two months after David's death wrapped around her. Slowly, the trembling subsided.

The bright sun that had warmed their skin in the kitchen had faded into dark shadows. The thunder rolling across the sky did not immediately register with Emily as she sat in the darkened bedroom, confronting the open drawers. Then she started. Thunder! In a flash, Emily remembered how his hand had melted in the stream of the shower.

In Emily's heated mind, thunder meant rain, and rain meant death. She didn't know what to make of the morning. It had been the stuff of such delightful and terrifying dreams. But as thunder crashed around her again, and droplets began to rattle the window, she sprang from the bed. If he got caught in the rain, her David, then she would lose him again.

She grabbed up a sundress that she had left pooled on the floor the night before. She threw it on, then raced to the door, slipped on a pair of slides and ran outside.

The rain was still intermittent by the time Emily reached street level and she looked frantically up and down the street, hoping to see his familiar silhouette sheltering beneath a doorway. Nothing. Frantically, she picked a direction, running toward the park. If she knew him, if he was her husband truly, then that was where he would go.

Doorways passed in a blur, faces turned aside but none of them were David. Rain came down harder, taking turns with her tears to blind her. She paused near the corner, dashing her hand across her eyes and squinting across. There—in the gazebo—a familiar silhouette? "David," she tried to yell, but emotion stifled her voice. She dashed toward the park boundary.

Emily noticed the car too late. She registered swift blue metal behind a brilliant flash of light as another clap of thunder rent the sky. And then the air was knocked from her lungs and she was on the ground, half lying on the sidewalk, half on the street. A warm body covered her own and held her tightly. Stunned, she opened her eyes.

"David," she moaned. "I'm sorry. I shouldn't have told you to leave." She reached a hand up to touch his face, still hovered protectively over hers. His smile was twisted in something like sorrow and relief. And then it morphed into pain. Her hand arrested and she stared up in horror as a thick glob of dough slid from the back of his neck, falling to pool in the hollow of her throat.

"No," she whispered, horrified. David stood, clapping a hand to his neck and screwing his face in pain as his skin bubbled and liquified in the steady rain. He took a shaky step back, then another. Too late, Emily noticed the railing behind him, realizing that they had tumbled by the bridge. David's body glided eerily smoothly along the railing, slipping up and over the edge. In the next moment, he was gone.

"No!" Emily's scream ripped from her core and she scrambled for the railing. The slick line of wet paste was already washing off the black iron barrier. She stared for a moment into the brackish water that was churning with the influx of sudden rain. Vaguely, she noticed people running toward her out of her periphery. They might have been shouting, but she could hear nothing at all beyond her bounding heart. She clutched the bar, took one last shrieking breath, and jumped.

The river was high and the bridge low, and Emily found herself immersed in water before she had time for any regrets. She found her way to the surface, spluttering, to find herself already past the bridge, carried by the current. She looked downstream, saw a streak of white marring the water, and set out swimming, desperate to catch up, hoping to catch anything at all.

She reached the skim of dough riding over the water and her heart collapsed. Already, the pattering rain was dissipating the thick, pale smudge. She rode in the current, her fingers swiping through the diminishing paste. The river continued to carry her through the city, and she had a sudden vision of herself sinking below the surface, hidden and quiet.

Something brushed her ankle. It was solid. It felt like a hand. Emily didn't hesitate; she dove. She came up with nothing, forced air into her lungs, and dove once more. This time, her searching fingers found an arm, found skin, brushed past hair. It was definitely a person. She curled one hand through the thick hair and another around an arm. Straining, she kicked, eyes open and trained on faint gray light that signaled the surface.

She kicked hard, breaking into the air. Rain shot down as hard as ever and she used her legs to propel the body up. Clasping her arms around the limp torso, she kicked toward a dock that jutted out into the water. By the time she reached the struts that supported the small dock, she was too tired to do more than dangle in the water, her cargo held desperately close. The body in her arms started and coughed. Her arm stretched as he inhaled hoarsely, and she cried out in relief as he began to stir.

"David?" she asked cautiously, unable to keep the tremble from her voice as tears once again threatened. The man she held in her arms stilled and slowly reached up to grab a strut of the dock. He turned and she gasped.

Her husband, one arm anchoring him to the dock, stared back at her, hair plastered by the rain and the river.

"Em," he whispered, his voice rough. His eyes widened in shock and he touched his hand to his throat in wonder. "You—" he cleared his throat. "You came for me. I—I came back."

"Yes, you came back." She gasped. "Your hand!"

Startled he held out his hand: five fingers and a palm. Emily grabbed it to prove to herself it was real. She pressed her lips into his wet, solid palm.

With a moan, he swept her into his arms and she noticed as he began to kiss her, that he tasted like David again. Emily sank into his kiss, letting the rushing water tangle their limbs as though they had never been apart. If there was still an edge of cinnamon to his lips, she couldn't complain.

ALL IN A DAY'S WORK

Saskia Walker

Faye toyed with two sets of handcuffs while she considered how best to handle the current situation. She was with an attractive merchant banker who was begging to be broken in. Faye—who was known as Faye the Bountiful amongst her closest friends—savored the anticipation. George, the merchant banker, watched her toy with the handcuffs with an eager look in his eye, waiting for her to take action. George didn't know what he was in for.

Her body simmered with arousal as she paced back and forth in front of him, eyeing him all the while. This was too much fun. The soft creak of her tight leather jeans and the click of her boot heels on the marble floor were the only sounds in the room. Sunlight poured through the floor-to-ceiling windows of George's city office, and she basked in it. These were the corridors of power, and the fact that she was there at all was quite a kick. As yet, she hadn't even used her magic on him, and his attention was all hers. George was an influential man, and if she hadn't been Faye the Bountiful her mind might have been moving in an altogether different direction, a more selfish one. But there was more to this than met the eye. Faye the Bountiful was a mischievous sort, and the situation compelled her to act in an unexpected way.

"Faye, please." George stared down at the handcuffs she had dangling from her hand, and swallowed. Tension was evident in his voice and posture. He was as taut as an arrow about to fly from its bow. The bulge at his groin was impressive.

"Patience, George." She gave him a quick smile. Having him at her mercy was intoxicating for them both, and there was a built-in thrill to getting him all hot and bothered during his lunch break, right there on his imported mahogany desk. "You know that it'll be worth the wait, don't you?"

"Oh, yes, you're worth it, but you're making me crazy here." He gave a low chuckle. "You goth women sure know how to make a man hard."

If he thought that was her secret, he was in for a big surprise.

His chest seemed to give a little tremor, right before her eyes. He was fit like an athlete with lean, toned muscles—the sort of man who worked out every morning.

"We wouldn't want to make you crazy, not when you have so many important things you have to do this afternoon."

What next? she mused. The belt on his expensive Yves Saint Laurent trousers was already hanging open. Faye had undone it. She had also removed his jacket, shirt and tie. She could strap him to his expensive flight-commander leather chair, tie him up against the marble pillar or splay him on the antique imported rug in front of the bookshelves.

He made a sound, something between a whimper and a bleat.

She closed on him, wrapped one hand around his neck and

kissed him, briefly. Then she lifted the papers from his desk, clearing them onto the adjoining computer table. With one fingernail, she tapped the surface of the desk.

George stepped closer to it. She circled him and then backed him against the edge of the desk. "Sit," she instructed.

He did so, and she rested one hand against his bare chest, easing him down. Then she lifted his hands in hers, pulling them over his head toward the opposite corner of the desk. Putting a cuff on each wrist, she secured both sets by dangling them down around the leg of the desk and then locking him in place. Returning to the other end of the desk, she stared down at him. His cock was pushing up beneath the zipper on his pants, the coins of his nipples tight and hard. Admiring the view, Faye smiled and nodded, letting him know that she approved of what she saw.

George cursed, his body arching up against the hard surface beneath him. He really got off on being dominated by women, and that fact fed into her awareness in the most delicious way, empowering her, making her instinctive magic flare. Right from the moment he'd brought her back to his office, walking her past his staff, she'd been on to the subtle underplay here. That atmosphere outside George's office was alive with interest, and Faye absorbed it all, quickly homing in on the true nature of the setup. "It's your lucky day, George," she'd said as she locked the door behind them and took charge of him, right there in his prestigious city offices. George had swallowed and nodded. He didn't know the half of it.

Allowing herself a couple of minutes to be sure she had the lay of the land, she determined her plan. Reaching for his button and the zipper on his trousers, she undid them slowly, watching as he urged her on with a pleading expression. Inside his trousers, his cock pushed against the soft white cotton of his jockey shorts. When she rested her hand over it, George groaned. The muscles in his arms tightened and he jerked at the restraints half-heartedly.

Easing down his jockey shorts, she let his cock bounce free. It was fully engorged and tapped eagerly against his rock-hard abs. "Poor George, you really want to come, don't you?"

His head turned to one side against the desk, his eyebrows lowering as he stared across his office at the door. "Yes."

The way he looked in that moment confirmed her feelings. She smiled to herself and clambered over him, kneeling on the desk, squeezing his thighs together with her knees. As she ran one finger up and down his breastbone, his cock twitched, his nice tight stomach tightening again before her eyes. Tension oozed from his every pore, and he stared at her with hungry eyes. Kneeling up at full stretch, she moved her hips in a slow circle, her leather jeans creaking as she did so. For her, the thrill was in sussing out what he really wanted. Outside his office, his staff speculated from desk to desk about what was going on in here. That was a big part of it for him. He'd made a show of bringing her in here, locking the door and asking not to be disturbed. Faye had also seen the way his secretary looked— crestfallen, to say the least—and she knew the speculation was running riot out there, and she was pretty sure that's what got him off.

"You trust me, don't you George?"

"You know that. I couldn't do this if I didn't." He paused, took a deep breath. "We agreed when we met, trust is impor-tant."

"Do you trust me to give you exactly what you want?" What he thought he wanted was to be bound and pleasured while everyone outside wondered what the hell was going on. There was more to it than that, and she'd figured it out.

"Do you believe I know what's best for you right now?"

His eyes flickered shut. Resistance was there, but after several long moments, he spoke. "Yes, I believe you probably do."

That was all that she needed to know.

"In that case, I'm going to give you what you really, really want." She stroked his jaw, bent over him and kissed his mouth softly good-bye.

Then she climbed off him and walked away. When she reached the door, she heard him whisper her name in a querying tone. She turned on her heel and looked back over her shoulder, arching one eyebrow at him. "You told me you trusted me."

He could easily have requested her not to leave his side. But he didn't. His body grew visibly tense, his cock jerking up against his abdomen. This was making him harder still. She restrained her smile.

"I do trust you," he whispered.

"Good."

Unlocking the door, she opened it and peeped out into the outer office. His secretary's desk was in a recessed bay four feet away, and she was staring right at Faye, wide eyed. Faye was willing to bet the poor woman never took her eyes off George's door when he was in there.

The open-plan office beyond the immediate area was busy and humming with noise. No one else seemed to have noticed the door was opening. It was too soon. Faye emerged as discreetly as she could.

The secretary lowered the pen she had been gnawing on as Faye approached.

Faye put her hands flat to the desk and leaned in close. "George is in there, half naked, and handcuffed to the desk. I'm leaving now."

The secretary's eyes rounded and her lips parted, her glance going back to the door. Despite the perfect cover of her immaculate makeup, color stained the secretary's cheeks.

Oh, yes, thought Faye, she'd been right about this one. The secretary was in her early thirties, and although she was pretty—with just the sort of blue-black hair her boss seemed to like—she dressed a mite too sedately for her own good. And she had a major crush on George.

"You have two options," Faye whispered.

Interest flared in the woman's eyes.

"You can go in there, make a fuss, and draw the attention of everyone in this room. He'll never live it down, and in all likelihood you will lose your job at some point not too long after today."

The secretary swallowed. "I wouldn't want that to happen."

"Of course not. However, you have a second option. I saw the way you looked at him, and—believe me—he is interested in you, too."

The secretary's pupils dilated.

"So your other option is to go in there quietly and lock the door behind you. Take charge of him, sexually. Believe me, he'll love it. He'd also love it if in future you dressed in black...you know, do the sexy power-dressing thing." Faye waggled her eyebrows and then reached into her hip pocket, fishing out the keys for the handcuffs. She put them on the desk. "You'll need these. I recommend you don't take the cuffs off until after you make him come."

The secretary looked down at the keys, glanced at the door to the office, and then looked back at Faye. "I don't know if I can," she murmured. "I mean, I knew *you*..." She paused. "But I don't know if I have the nerve."

"Of course you do. I bet you've thought about doing it, haven't you?"

"Oh, yes, especially once I knew George was into...that." The color on her cheekbones darkened.

"Just keep your chin up, and take charge." Faye ran her fingers over the back of the woman's hand, infusing her with enough erotic magic to empower her, ensuring that the secretary would take action on her secret desires. "I guarantee you'll find it very rewarding." Faye winked. "You'll have him eating out of your palm before your afternoon tea break, believe me. You might even get a raise."

The secretary nodded, one hand pressed to her collarbone to quell her excitement as she looked at the door to George's office, a smile lifting the corners of her mouth. Her job done, Faye straightened her leather jacket and headed off. By the time she'd weaved her way across the open-plan office and pressed the call button for the elevator, the secretary was tentatively walking into George's office. Faye watched until she closed the door behind her, firmly. It stayed shut.

As she stepped into the mirrored elevator, Faye was pleased to find she was on her own. As the doors closed behind her, she let out a deep sigh, and her magic shimmered around her. In the mirror facing her she could see her aura gleam purple, filled with mischief and sexual power. Lowering her hand to her groin, she clasped the mound of her pussy through her leather jeans and squeezed hard, rocking into her hand, seeking her own relief.

Well, she had to grab the chance while she could; her job was an arousing one.

Closing her eyes, she spirited herself back to George's office, peeping in on her erotic matchmaking—just to ensure it was on the right track and that she wasn't needed to push this thing along any more. When her spirit fluttered into the room— invisible to the human eye but for a purple wisp of light—she found George's secretary standing by his desk, one hand running down his chest until she reached his upright cock. George's mouth moved and the head of his cock darkened. A moment later, the secretary hitched her skirt up around her hips, dropped her panties to the floor and clambered onto the desk, mounting him eagerly.

If Faye had any doubts about her instinct on this one, they vanished in that moment. She chuckled gleefully to herself and watched a moment longer—long enough to see the secretary sinking gratefully onto George's erection; long enough to see George arch up from the desk to meet her; long enough to see the secretary throwing her head back with joy as she impaled herself on his shaft, and long enough to make herself come. Her hips rolled and a sweet orgasm blossomed inside her.

The elevator pinged.

Donning her sunglasses, Faye breathed in her purple aura just as the elevator doors slid open, and stepped out into the busy foyer. A moment later she walked out onto the city street and passed through the crowds, eyeing the people, looking for the next lucky person who might need a dose of her mischievous erotic magic.

It was all in a day's work for this particular fairy god-mother.

BIG BAD WOLF
(AN EXCERPT)

Alana Noël Voth

Dillon wakes to his dog barking. He gets out of bed, goes to a window, and then pulls back a curtain and sees Segar barking at something in the lot outside his trailer. Dillon stares through the glass, then sees the other dog, a big dog with silver-white fur.

Dillon hurries to the front door and opens it before staring through the screen.

The other dog isn't a dog. It's a wolf.

Dillon shouts, "Segar, come here!"

The wolf jerks its head in Dillon's direction. Segar keeps barking. Dillon calls his dog again. The wolf looks at Segar and then at Dillon in the doorway. Since when do wolves venture this close to civilization? Even if Dillon's place is out of the way, aren't wolves shy? Maybe the wolf is a hybrid, someone's great idea for a pet.

Goddamn, the thing is big.

Dillon opens the screen door. "Segar! Come here!" He steps

onto the landing not sure how far to go. His rifle is in the shed.

The wolf regards him beneath the awning in his boxer shorts then trots across the gravel lot into the tree line and disappears. Segar meets Dillon on the landing. The man holds his dog's head in his hands. "Hey, boy, what the hell was that, huh?"

At noon, Dillon heads for his truck. At the edge of the trees, the wolf lies in the shade, watching him. Dillon gets in his truck and drives across the gravel lot toward the bar he owns watching the wolf become smaller and smaller in his rearview mirror.

In town, a woman in the grocery store says, "You own Segar's up the road, right?"

Dillon nods.

"Yeah, the bar and grill. I heard it was fun." The woman has a soft smile, dark eyes.

"Yeah, I hope it is," Dillon says.

The woman puts his milk in a bag. "I'll come by sometime."

"That would be great." Dillon's never sure when women are flirting with him. Yeah, they flirted. He wasn't a bad-looking guy if you didn't mind T-shirts and jeans, flannel in the winter and cowboy boots no matter the weather. Dillon wore his hair longish, and he didn't always shave, meaning he didn't mind a quarter-inch of whiskers. Women had told him, *You're rugged but cute.* Another thing, he was shy, since he was a kid, since forever, chunks of his childhood missing too.

His parents had left him with his grandparents when he was four.

"Bye, Dilly." He remembered his mother with blue eyes. He'd wanted to ask her where she was going but didn't. Dillon had a vague recollection of his father's voice. "Dillon, stand up straight." Dillon got a flash of himself in a corner with his arms around a dog. But what Dillon remembered most from childhood was his grandfather, Segar Blackhawk Curtis. He'd taken Dillon into the mountains, into the snow.

They'd sat around campfires, gutted and grilled fish.

Dillon pays for his groceries. The woman gives him his bags. They make eye contact. Dillon looks away.

"Hey, thanks. Have a great day."

When he returns from town the wolf is still by the trees. Dillon gets out of his truck. The wolf gets to its feet. Dillon walks toward the house. The wolf is white against the tree line. It's clean, not ragged or muddy or starved looking. At the steps in front of the trailer Dillon stops and looks again. The wolf is gone.

Later in the bar, Dillon sees Ray Shepherd. He and some other men have gathered at the pool tables. They've ordered several pints of beer. They're suntanned men who work construction. Ray clenches a cigarette in his teeth. Dillon allows his patrons to smoke in the bar, never mind state regulations or whatever bullshit.

He asks Ray, "You heard about a wolf in these parts lately?"

"Not in fourteen years," Ray answers.

Dillon thinks about the wolf outside his house.

Another guy speaks up. "May Wagner says she saw a wolf four days ago."

"She saw a coyote," Ray says then leans over the pool table. He knocks a ball in the upper left pocket and walks around the table. "She can't keep track of her kids running around like raccoons is all. She's paranoid." Ray leans in for another shot, makes it. "If there's a wolf around here we'll call Sarah Palin, see if we can't get her permission for a hunt."

"Nice rug to go with your stuffed cougar," says another of Ray's friends.

A couple of the men toast.

Ray cocks a brow. "I wouldn't get too excited. Palin ain't got jurisdiction around here. In these parts, wolves are an endangered species."

"Yeah, so is pussy," another guy says.

The men laugh. Ray lands one in a side pocket.

"Aren't wolves endangered in Alaska?" Dillon says.

Ray chuckles. "Who knows? It's all a popularity contest, right, politics?"

"Yeah, probably." Dillon says good night to the men.

The last waitress cashes out at one-thirty. Dillon locks the vault. Outside the bar, Dillon stands in the night air and listens to a truck pulling out of the gravel parking lot.

As he walks to his trailer, Dillon sees something move across the darkness and stops. The wolf is a few yards off when Dillon reaches his trailer.

When he was kid, his grandfather used to tell him you could see your conscience on the night like glints of silver on fish scales.

At four a.m., Segar wants out. Dillon opens the back door of the trailer. "Don't go too far, all right?" The dog disappears in the trees.

"Segar," Dillon calls him. After a while, Dillon lets the door swing shut. The dog would be back, of course. Dillon falls onto the bed again, hugs a pillow.

At ten a.m. Dillon stands in his bathroom staring at himself in a mirror. He's not a big guy: thin, a little muscular in his arms and chest. He combs his hands though his hair. Five years now he'd been in Colorado, fifty miles west of Denver, deep in the mountains, quiet for the most part, and green. His grandfather's people had been mountain people, had weathered blizzards and lived off elk. They'd been grateful to all animals, his grandfather had told him, for their sacrifices, their meat and skins.

Be grateful, his grandfather had said.

"Okay, Grandpa."

Dillon used to thank the goldfish in his classroom, a spider stringing its web between branches, stray dogs.

Now Dillon owned a bar that paid respect to his grandfather. Dillon had money in the bank and wasn't so far from Montana where'd he grown up. He got lonely sometimes though and had taken up with the help before, not to mention women who came to the bar. Why not? He couldn't say his grandparents had been religious. Spiritual, yeah, in touch with nature, sure. Dillon's grandfather had spoken to him about reincarnation, multiple dimensions and souls leaving bodies to experience alternate existences, and Dillon had appreciated his grandfather's assertions even if he hadn't believed it all.

He liked the idea of second chances though.

After a shower, Dillon sits in the kitchen doing a crossword puzzle in pencil because he hates how if he makes a mistake he can't change it if he's written the answer in ink. Nothing, he thinks, should be etched in stone or permanent. If his mother ever turned up again, he'd hug her. If his father showed up, Dillon would welcome him, too.

When Dillon pours his third cup of coffee, something comes on the radio about a woman seeing a wolf in her backyard and how it had gotten too close to one of her kids, a three-year-old boy who'd wandered out of the yard toward the river.

Jesus Christ, Dillon thinks, *May Wagner.*

Outside, Segar starts barking. Dillon looks through a window and doesn't see anything but his collie barking his head off, before he realizes the wolf is out there, too.

Dillon opens the front door and steps onto the landing. Segar leaps in the air, barking. The wolf sees Dillon and heads into the trees. His dog follows. Dillon doesn't call Segar back. He sits on the step. The sky is blue; the air isn't hot yet, and his truck could use a wash. Dillon pulls his shirt off over his head then goes to get a hose and bucket; he grabs soap from the house then comes back out and starts the water. He lets the water spray over him. Segar comes back later. The wolf isn't with him.

"Where is she?" Dillon says.

He feeds the dog kibble. He isn't sure what a wolf eats, besides him that is. Dillon chuckles. History lacked documented cases of wolves attacking, let alone eating people, although folks made shit up, old wives' tales, superstition and disgruntled ranchers. Capitalism was the best reason for wiping out a species.

Dillon goes inside the house and cooks a piece of meat. He calls Segar into the house and leaves the meat outside before heading into the bar for work.

The woman from the grocery store is there. Her hair shines; she has that same soft smile. Dillon wants to push his face in her hair, smell her. She gives him her number, which he pushes into his pocket. When Dillon comes out of the bar later, the wolf lies at the foot of the steps in front of his trailer. Dillon isn't sure about the meat, if it's there or not. He thinks she's eaten it though. Inside the house, Segar is barking.

"You going to let me by or what?"

Dillon waits before taking a step forward. The wolf gets up and takes a step backward. They're five feet apart. Once he gets to the landing, Dillon turns around.

"See you in the morning."

He lets Segar out at five a.m. No sign of the wolf. Later, Dillon sits at the front window drinking coffee. Segar comes back alone. At noon, one of the beer distributors shows up, and Dillon helps the guy unload beer off the truck. They carry the cases into the bar and then line the beer on shelves in a walk-in cooler. The other guy talks about the Denver Broncos and a shortage of good women in their surrounding area.

When they're outside, Dillon looks toward the tree line.

The distributor takes a pack of cigarettes from his shirt pocket.

"Want one?"

"Nah, thanks." Dillon stares at the trees and sees nothing but trees.

"You hear about the dead chickens they're finding all over the place?"

"What?" Dillon looks at the guy.

The guy lights a cigarette. "Farmers are complaining some animal is getting all their chickens. Most say a coyote or fox, but a few are claiming it's a wolf." The guy sucks the end of his cigarette then exhales. "You didn't hear any of that, huh?"

"Nah, didn't hear any of it."

Later, Dillon leaves more meat out for the wolf.

Later than that, he runs into the woman from the grocery store again. He's behind the bar helping his bartender.

"Hey, Mia. How are you?"

She leans into the bar, showing cleavage. "Can I get a shot of whiskey, Dillon?"

"Sure." He feels heated. Dillon pours her one.

"Thanks, sweetie."

She leaves lipstick on her glass. The bar gets busy. Dillon ends up in the kitchen helping his cooks. The waitresses dash between tables. Dillon moves between the kitchen and the bar. When he gets a chance, he walks the floor and thanks people for coming. He smiles at Mia when he sees her. At closing, she's waiting for him.

"I told my friends to go on without me."

Dillon breathes a sigh of relief. "Give me a couple minutes, okay?"

"Okay." Mia walks toward the jukebox. She has a way of walking. Mia puts money into the machine and then Buffalo Springfield starts to sing, *Something's happening here...*

Back in his office, Dillon cashes the waitresses out, tries not to hurry. One of the cooks teases him about getting lucky. He walks with Mia to his trailer. He keeps his hands in his pockets. Inside the trailer Dillon pushes a hand through his hair.

"How long has it been?" she says.

"I don't know... What do you mean?"

"You know what I mean."

Dillon feels himself blush. "A while, I guess." He shouldn't have admitted that.

Mia grabs him by the back of his head and kisses him. On the couch, Dillon lies between her legs then pushes his mouth to her neck. She smells like perfume and whiskey. Dillon dry-humps her. He moves his hand inside her blouse then hears a thump against the front door. Another.

"What was that?" Mia goes still beneath him.

Dillon looks up, shakes his head. "Don't know."

Something paws at the screen door, tearing at it really.

"Jesus Christ!" Mia sits up beneath him. "What the hell is it?"

Dillon gets up. The noise stops. Dillon opens the door. Half the screen door is gone. Dillon pushes his hand through his hair, waits a second. Nothing there. He eases what's left of the screen door open. Everything's quiet. Mia comes up behind him.

"What's going on?"

Dillon hears the growling, maybe from under the steps.

"Did you hear something?" Mia says.

Dillon puts his finger to his mouth. Mia looks at him. They both wait a minute.

"I'll walk you to your car," Dillon says.

"What?"

"It'll be okay."

Mia's frightened but doesn't want to leave. "Okay, let's both go," she says.

Dillon grabs her hand then pulls her across the lot between his trailer and the bar.

"Where you parked?" he says.

Mia points. She grabs hold of his arm. So close but so far away.

At her car, Dillon helps her in. Mia looks at him. "Aren't you coming?"

Dillon leans in the window then kisses her on her lips. She tastes like something he's had before: regret or reluctance...but that couldn't be it. He has to get going. Mia grabs him by the back of his head, kisses him back. Dillon pulls away from the window.

"Drive safe, okay?"

He steps away from the car. Mia turns the ignition. Dillon heads across the parking lot and takes a big breath. Something moves, slipping into formation.

"Guess I'm headed to Home Depot tomorrow, huh? Nice job on the screen. You hungry?"

Dillon goes inside the trailer, screen door hanging on its hinges, then takes meat from the refrigerator, heats a pan, and then grills a piece of meat before tossing it to the wolf under his kitchen table.

She follows him as far as outside his bedroom door. One morning, when he's in the shower, she goes into the bedroom and lies at the foot of his bed. When he comes into the bedroom with a towel around his waist, she smells the soap on him, his skin, the blood underneath; she can hear him breathing.

"Hey," he says, and for the first time he crouches so he's at her level.

He has dark blond hair on his legs. She smells the musk of his asshole, salt on his balls. Dillon holds his hand out. She stands and walks forward. He keeps his hand open, palm up. Dillon feels the wolf's nose against his fingertips and then her fur in his hand.

He touches her head, behind her ears, her neck. She has blue eyes.

She watches him repair the door. "Christ," he says, "You did a number on this thing, didn't you?" Dillon shakes his head. "Nobody has heard of a wolf in these parts for fourteen years." Dillon stops his work to look at her. "Want to tell me how you got here?" After a minute he says, "Fuck, like you're going to answer."

She follows him around the trailer, outside in the lot, but never into the bar. While Dillon works, the wolf runs with Segar through the woods. The wolf outruns the dog then finds the chickens and bites their necks, eats them. She kills and eats cats too, nothing wasted. From the dark she stares into lighted windows at children. She licks the dirt children leave behind them, the taste of the soles of their feet.

One night, Dillon gets drunk at the bar. He's in a bad mood: maybe because he can't find Mia's number. Okay, so what if he liked her? Dillon drinks one more whiskey. Later, he makes it through the door to his trailer. The wolf follows him into his bedroom. Without looking at her, Dillon throws off his clothes and then falls onto the bed.

After a minute, he feels the weight of the wolf beside him.

"Ah, what?" Dillon drops his hand onto the wolf's back and then pushes his fingers through her fur, feels for her spine, presses the edges. He passes out.

Segar wakes him whining. Dillon tries to ignore the noise then manages to open one eye then another. "Shit," he says. "Let yourself out."

Dillon sits up. Beside him on the bed is a naked woman. Dillon is sure of it, except he isn't sure if he'd brought home a woman. He has to think, had he brought a woman home? She has blonde hair, long to her waist. He can't see her face.

Segar whines again then backs toward the door.

"All right, all right," he says.

Dillon gets off the bed then goes to the backdoor to let the dog out. Segar takes off. Dillon remembers the wolf. No sign of her now. There's a woman in his bed. He should get back there. Dillon returns to his bedroom; the woman's still on the bed, the shape of her there. The woman sits up and looks at him. She's beautiful, holy Christ. Dillon goes to the bed then lowers himself beside her. He looks at her, smells something on her, the trees outside, something. She leans in and kisses him on his mouth. Her saliva is hot; her tongue fills his mouth. Dillon grabs the back of her head. She pushes him onto his back and straddles him. His cock is hard. She maneuvers him into her. Dillon arches beneath her, spits a breath through his lips, comes. She climbs off him, pushes her nose into his armpit. Dillon lets his eyes slide shut.

It's daylight. Dillon stands beside the bed; the woman is curled around his pillow, still sleeping. Probably he should figure this out or at least feel suspicious. Maybe he should tell her to leave. How could he want her to leave? You don't look a gift horse in its mouth, do you? Dillon wipes his brow.

Outside the bedroom window, Segar barks. Dillon goes to feed the dog then sits on the steps and watches Segar tear into his kibble. The dog looks at him.

"Don't look at me like that," Dillon says.

He goes inside the house, makes coffee, starts bacon and eggs.

Dillon turns from the stove and there she is.

"Hi," he says.

She crosses the kitchen, then she puts her arms around his neck and hugs him. Dillon feels her naked body through his jeans, against his bare chest. She kisses the line of his jaw, the tender part of his neck.

"Hey," he says but doesn't push her away. He pulls her closer.

The woman kisses his mouth. Dillon opens it to her, how can he resist? She pulls at the front of his jeans. Dillon lifts her onto the kitchen counter, fucks her like that.

Later, she eats bacon and eggs with her bare hands.

"What's your name?" Dillon says.

She has bacon grease smeared across her mouth; she doesn't answer.

When he has to go to work later Dillon says, "Stay here," because he's afraid he'll come home and she will have disappeared.

She doesn't stay.

While Dillon is in the kitchen helping his cooks, she wanders into the bar.

A waitress happens to comment while she's waiting for an order: "A girl in nothing but a shirt and cowboys boots has got the boys going at the pool table."

Immediately, Dillon goes to investigate. There, by the pool table, she wears one of his flannel shirts, a pair of his boots.

When she leans over the pool table, the shirt hikes up and reveals the bottom curve of her hip. Dillon rushes across the bar. She goes to him, boots slapping the floor, and hugs him.

Dillon takes hold, holds her close.

"Your girl, Curtis?" Ray backs up respectfully but still looks at her. How could he not? She was a bit barbaric, lupine-like even, but beautiful.

Dillon holds her face in his hands. "You okay?"

She kisses his mouth.

"Lucky bastard," another guy says.

"You all right?" Dillon looks at her, can't let go of her, stares in her eyes and sees the yellow rims around the blue of her irises.

She pulls her head from his hands.

"She sure can play pool," Ray says.

Come here, Dillon wants to say. His hands ache. "What do you want to do?" Dillon imagines gathering her hair in his hands. He imagines she curls up on the rug in his office. He shudders once. She goes back to the pool table and picks up a cue stick.

After he closes the bar, they walk across the lot. Dillon squeezes her hand in his. She's there, she's real. In the trailer, she takes off his shirt, pulls his boots off. She kisses him all the way up the inside of his legs. She takes his balls in her mouth. She sucks him. Dillon shudders. He smells pine in her hair, earth. He sees a flash of white in the air, her teeth. She's smiling at him before taking him into her mouth again. Before he can come, Dillon is on his knees between her legs as she lies on his bed. He kisses the inside of her knees, the inside of her thighs; he holds her legs with his hands. He pushes his face into the center of her, running his tongue over her cunt, pulling on her with his lips, pushing his tongue inside her. He wants to be the one to make her come.

She holds the sheet on each side of her and feels her legs tremble. She takes a breath, sinks into it. After she comes she sits up and looks at him.

"Hi, Dillon."

He remembers the first time he saw three rainbows at once. He recalls the glow of colors and a raw taste of rain. He tastes her cunt on his tongue now, then hears her say his name. He mounts her as if to hurry: she'll slip through his arms, the trees, disappear.

"Don't leave me," he says.

She nuzzles his neck, bites him. He comes before he's aware of the pain.

THE KISS

Michelle Augello-Page

And they lived happily after. That was the first lie she learned, long, long ago, when she was a child of light, a dream living in a sun-drenched room, waiting for the one who would come and rescue her from a world that offered no more fairy tales.

He had met her in a dark club, past midnight, as the moon hid behind nocturnal clouds. He wouldn't have remembered the sky, but she had told him that she only went out dancing when the moon stirred within her. They danced by each other, and he was captivated by her ruthlessness, the way the hard music entered her body and was released in movement. He did not touch her. Later, outside, she approached him and kissed his lips, her mouth stained with Southern Comfort and cigarette smoke.

"Who are you?" she asked.

"If I told you that, you would never believe me."

"Then lie," she said, shading her eyes from the stars.

"My tale has become tainted with the blackness of the earth, the darkness of the sky. I have no body; I take what is not mine in the dreams of night, the nightmares of loss at the edges of what should never be." He looked at her plainly, his eyes reflecting nothing. "I'm sorry, you told me to lie."

"And yet, I believe you."

They laughed. He remembered her laugh, light and airy; belying the weight he sensed surrounding her as an aura.

He looked in the mirror; her eyes were lined with black, her lashes brushed with midnight. Her hair fell around her shoulders as if they were being licked by fire. He surveyed her body: her breasts were soft, her arms thin, her thighs full. He ran his hands along the line of her abdomen, feeling the round of her belly, the hard places of bone. He liked this body, though it was not flawless. He would become intimate with each of its scars, purposeful and accidental, lines of cuts, childhood stitches, designs colored with black ink. The time had come to travel again.

"Take me home." She did not ask. He would later remind himself; it was what she had wanted.

After mother died and father became lost in the eye of a fractured bottle, Danae ran away, far from the idyllic wood that held magic just within reach, the place where she grew from a child into a young woman, the place of secret passages and locked doors. She ran as far as the wind swept her, into the city, and found the world she suspected existed on the other side, framed by long and jagged shadows.

He smiled and brushed strands of hair from her eyes.

"What's your name?" he whispered.

"Danae."

"Pretty name," he said. "And were you locked in a brazen tower by your father after a prophecy foretold?"

"Ah, you know mythology, but did you ever see some of the paintings?"

"I only know the one by Klimt." He looked at her again,

reconciling her image to the sudden recollection of the painting, seeing the echo of the sensual turn of her mouth, the casual sexuality of her captured glance.

"Of course," she said, sensing his growing awareness, "it's not my true name."

"Neither is mine."

"But you haven't told me yours yet," she laughed.

"Give me a name," he said.

She looked at him, head titled, surveying the minutiae of his features. She stepped back and then took the length of his body in her glance. Through his black silk shirt his arms gave the appearance of being finely chiseled. For a second she felt as if his eyes did not match his body. His eyes...they were so deep they seemed ancient, in contrast with the accidental youth and beauty of his form.

"Your eyes are shocking."

"Oh?" He shifted, and veiled the expression on his face so quickly that she did not catch his unease at her statement.

"This is difficult." Danae laughed, and then grew serious, looking at him intently as he focused his eyes on the cracked asphalt outside the club, looking over the stained tar, spilled beer and crushed cigarettes littering the pavement.

"I suppose it has to be Gustav. Or Klimt, if you engender such formality."

"How about Zeus?"

"What ego," she countered, playfully hitting his arm.

"If you insist," he answered, "though I confess I lack both genius and creativity, and I am not a painter."

"That's okay," she smiled, "I am." Her smile fell briefly as she corrected herself. "Or I was."

"What do you paint?" he asked.

"Hmm," she began, "what can't be verbalized even if I

wanted to use words to describe its meaning, what is unknowable, the space between thought and action, shades of gray, negative prisms, shadows...but I...I can't...I've lost whatever impulse I once had. It is as though I have been blinded. It's as if whatever once tethered me to the universe has been cut, and I have no sense of gravity. I no longer walk this life. I float."

Her dreams were sketches in charcoal, and her days were spent, wasted. As a child, her entire life was molded upon one quest: to be beautiful and kind, to await patiently her prince. The girl who once shone in the sun found her only solace in dreams, waiting, listening, refusing to believe the empty footsteps of her nightmares. She told her story in image and color. But Danae was not patient. When it became clear that no one would rescue her, she flung herself into the world. She learned how to find men who would never be princes, and she would stay with them as long as she could, until the next fix, until the next black and blue, until she could no longer.

"And what do you do?" she asked.

He wavered. He felt too close. He enjoyed talking to this woman; perhaps he would enjoy courting her, spending time with her. Perhaps, he thought bitterly, he could if he did not bear his fate. She was looking at him curiously, waiting for a clever answer, one that would continue their flirtation. His resistance was shallow and dissipated under her expectant smile. He wanted her. Damn him, he cursed himself, how he wanted her.

"I do," he answered, turning and smiling at her, "everything."

"That's exactly what I wanted to hear," she laughed.

Her laugh was a tinkling of bells, the distant knell of a cathedral, and again he was grasped with the feeling of not wanting to take her; he would rather confess to her in the dim light of a screened window, hide her in a cloistered place where everything was pure, where she would never be hurt again.

She used her body as a negligible thing, arms and legs and neck poised askew, standing on a shifting precipice, waiting, wanting desperately to fall. This life had betrayed her; it was nothing she had ever imagined when she looked at the stars, unaware of the immensity of the surrounding blackness. But he was hungry; he had outgrown the body of the vacant boy, that man-child who came to him when he was the raven-haired mistress, and before that the androgynous blonde. His thoughts faltered and his mind began to spiral, the wheel of his archaic soul beginning to turn. What would release him, who would allow his own return, where was his chance to begin again, anew?

As if she could sense his hesitation, she grasped his elbow. "It is time."

Upon entering the dark room, he lit a candle that stood on a small table. His apartment was modest and severe. It consisted of one large room and a small bathroom. There were no windows, the walls were painted white and a low beige carpet extended across the hardwood floor. There was no other furniture except for a bed.

"You don't really live here do you?" she said. "I like it better this way." She stood before him. He closed his eyes.

"Take off your dress," he said.

He knelt before her and opened her legs. Raising his face toward her shaved pubis, he began to taste her sex. She tensed her body and lifted her chin, releasing a deep sigh. His tongue thrust into her as he grasped her hips. He sucked her hard, running his hands up past her waist to her breasts. Her nipples were erect and he squeezed them tightly with his thumbs and forefingers. She moaned softly. He began to come upward, licking her stomach and then her chest. He took each breast into his mouth ravenously and bit her nipples, moving his hand between her legs, his fingers working her breath into a rasp, and then stopped.

"Do you know what I am?" His eyes bore into hers, allowing her to explore the depth of his need, his ambivalence, his desire. She met his gaze. He felt no fear from her.

"Why do you think I followed you outside and kissed you? I have waited for you, you without face or name. Of course I know you. I prayed for the universe to conspire with me to find you."

He moved away from her and watched her close her eyes. He knew he could do anything he wanted with her. He felt his own fever rising with the thought of her willful submission and his rising potency. This was the only way he could save her; he could restore her. He would open the pathway to the world's dream. He would release her.

"I want your body," he said.

"And I want yours," she answered.

"You can't have mine," he said, teasingly.

She smiled and began to unbutton his shirt. She ran her fingers along his lean and smooth chest, his hardness with a hint of musculature. Her mouth found his shoulder and neck and began to suck and bite his dark skin. She unbuckled his belt and liberated it from the loops of his pants, then she eased his hands behind him and tightened the belt across his wrists.

"My turn," she said as she went down on him, holding his smooth balls with her hands and penetrating her mouth with his penis. He was long and thick and hard, and she felt the pure pleasure of his maleness, desperately wanting him inside her. One hand stroked his perineum while the other circled his anus; then she pressed her fingertips against him, sliding within as she sucked him, teeth and tongue and breath.

He freed himself from his loose restraints and grabbed her

hair, gently. She withdrew as he pulled her to standing and crushed his body against hers. He entered her standing, her pussy throbbing and wet with desire, his penis swollen and rigid. He tore into her and she moaned with pleasure. He pulled her legs upward as she tightened around him; he held her full weight in the air, pushing slowly, mercilessly inside her.

"Harder," she said, lowering her head and torso backward and reaching toward the floor with her hands.

Driving within her, he fucked her harder, faster, until she weakened.

"Don't come," he instructed, and lowered himself toward the ground, pulling her toward him, still thrusting into her deeply, as she positioned herself on top of him. He lay backward on the floor, urging her closer, as he kissed her roughly. She slowed her movements, feeling his penis erect and full, closer and closer to the edge of orgasm, that rising place she wanted more than anything to succumb to.

"Please…" she whispered, begging seductively.

Still rocking inside of her, he reached for the belt. She maneuvered her body astride him so that her back was to him, while reaching for his cock with her hands. She massaged her anus with her wetness and pressed herself against the head of his penis. He tied her hands behind her back, pulling the belt through the buckle so that it secured her wrists. He pulled it tightly and she moaned, "Yes," falling onto all fours as he entered her from behind, gently at first, as the opening made way for him, then more steadily. She raised her buttocks into the air as he swung inside her, rubbing her clitoris with his thumb and smoothing in and out of her pussy with his fingers. "Don't come." he said, and she cried out. But she could not refuse him.

"You like it?" he asked, breathing the words, dripping with heat and sweat.

She could barely speak, she moaned, "*Yes, yes.*"

"You want to come, don't you? It will be sweet, so, so sweet. Tell me I can have your body. I will release you into a pleasure so deep and complete you will leave this mortal plane."

She moaned and sighed, closer.

Danae was once a child of light, a beauty stripped, locked in a bare room. Mother died, leaving her father steeped in whiskey and smoke, crawling in the shadows of night. Perhaps there would be one to replace the wound, but she had learned some secrets from the forest; she knew it would never heal. So she ran. She dyed her spun-gold hair red as flame, she carved her story into her skin, she forgot the language of the wind and sky, and then she forgot the words, spelled in ways she could barely whisper.

"Say 'you can have my body.'"

Images of a painting destroyed in fire, awash with the golden hue of the sun. Body upon body, flesh upon bone, and a single blessed space. Skull, fur, skin. Hygeia holding a snake and a cup from the river Lethe. Time, torment, bliss.

"You can have my body," she moaned, twisting, panting, aching under his enchantment and then released into climax, a pleasure so pure that her whole body shook with it, enraptured, free, falling. He caught her in his embrace and held her so close, so completely, their bodies entwined in glistening gold. There was only a moment; he reached for her tranquil face, upturned and angled, and strained his neck and shoulder to place upon her cheek a kiss.

The kiss, and then he was alone, slick with sex and transformation. Her body his, once upon a time.

THE RETURN

Charlotte Stein

I panic when I hear he's coming back. Of course I do. All I can see is the heavy dull shape of him in the corner of our bedroom, waiting for me to die of boredom. Those stultifying hours together, filling time up with nothing; meals I'd made that went uneaten, silence thick as treacle.

I don't know why things aren't boring anymore. I guess being alone should have made things worse, but in many ways it hasn't. I always eat my own meals, and I never stand in the corner of my bedroom, waiting, and every single day I get to watch whatever I want on the television. If I choose, I can read a book. There's no one here to say anything about it.

Sometimes I just sit out on the deck and watch the waves with a glass of something I shouldn't drink in my hands. I do it until the sunset is bloody and loaded on the horizon, and night comes in like Roland returning.

* * *

It wasn't that Roland was cruel. He didn't beat me or stop me from doing anything. It's just that everything he wanted lay like a blanket over our lives—the scratchy, heavy sort of blanket that you fall asleep under by accident and then can't seem to escape from—half awake, limbs flailing, everything seeming too hot and sweaty.

That was my life with Roland, and now he's back from business in Japan after what seems like years, and I don't want to go back under the covers. I don't want to, no matter how terrible and ungrateful that is. He pays for this house, this lifestyle, this everything for god's sake.

Pull yourself together, Margot.

I pull myself together all right. I lace myself up so tight I can hear my joints squeak when I move. I greet him at the door with an immobilized face, lumbering like Frankenstein's monster because my feet don't seem to want to get away from each other. If I barely move, then I don't have to answer the door or say hello or worse yet—hug him.

But he's here, now, and I have to. My stiff robot's arms, laced tight at the elbows, reach out for him. My mouth stretches into a smile.

When he clasps me to him, I feel the blanket descend.

But then things don't seem quite right for my blanket-living life. At first I try to pretend they are, until I get to a certain point and I know that I have to stop. Pretending, I mean. I've pretended so hard that I've missed things that seem very obvious, when I look back on them with new eyes.

Like the way he smelled, at the door. Not of something bland and gray, but spicy instead. Even in that robotic hug and with all my senses trying to close off, I could almost taste that smell.

It had stayed with me all the way up to the bathtub, where I'd soaked long and hard to get him off of me.

Now I wonder why I let it go so easily. I can hardly remember what that new smell was like, or even if it was real, and it's not like I can just go up to him and hug him to show myself how real it was. But without the hug it's hard to catch that scent. That scent of someone *new*.

And then there's the way he looked at the door—and still looks now. There's something about it…something too put together. Roland was always neat, always be-suited and tied, but this is different somehow. It's too…careful.

He looks at me sly eyed from across the dinner table, in his too careful clothes and with that too careful hair. I'm sure Roland never used to side-part it in quite that way—severely, but without the Brylcreem.

And there's another thing about this new Roland that he doesn't think I know: he smokes.

I suppose I should be concerned by these developments. Smoking makes a person worse, not better, right? Especially *secret* smoking that he thinks I don't know about. Especially when Roland was *never* the kind of person to smoke. He hates smokers. Smokers put unnecessary pressure on the economy and do not care about their own physical well-being. Smokers should do more yoga.

But this new Roland doesn't seem to give a rat's ass what smokers should and should not do. Instead he chews a lot of spearmint gum and gargles a lot of mouthwash, and pretends he doesn't smoke.

But I know, because I'm watching him. I watch him getting ready for bed. He's skinnier than he used to be—just as perfectly muscled and poised, of course, but noticeably skinnier. The thick bones of his shoulders stand out like a gleaming round newel post. I can see the heavy rails of his ribs when he bends over.

And then he turns and asks, "Why are you staring?"

I'm staring, I think, *because you are not Roland.*

It has taken me a while to come to this conclusion, but now that I'm there it's more of a relief than I would have guessed. I don't feel insane. It's just a fact, like washing on Wednesdays and red going with black. He doesn't act like Roland, he doesn't smell like Roland, he's like a ghost in his own house. He hasn't even tried to fuck me yet, and I know Roland would have.

Flat on my back, thirty seconds of missionary: I was almost looking forward to it.

"I wasn't," I say, but I suppose we both know differently. I think he definitely knows differently, because now he's stood half in and out of the dim light from the bathroom, gazing at me darkly with eyes that are not Roland's.

He could just cross that small space and get his hands around my throat, quickly, before anyone else realizes he is an impostor. I shiver, thinking of those big strange hands on me. I shiver in my little cotton nightgown, wondering how I look to this stranger. Soft, do I look soft? Do I look like a sweetly appealing wife, ready to give in to her fake husband's needs?

Or is he just waiting for me to attack? Struggle, spit, try to escape?

He is vaguely stroking one too-long sideburn, but then he lets his hand drop. He walks toward me, slow and rolling—like a predator might.

I don't move from the corner of the bed. I don't even plant my feet down on the carpet, as though I'm about to run. I can feel my chest trying to heave with the pressure my lungs and heart are putting on it, but I resist. It's just my husband, crossing the carpet to his wife. It's nothing.

He puts a hand on my shoulder and I press my lips together

hard enough to hurt. I can't look at him. I keep my eyes trained on his navel, while he strokes said hand over the strap of my nightgown. He strokes until it falls —almost exposing my right breast—and then he runs his fingers over the skin of my shoulder. Nothing more. Just there, with his thick rough thumb coming close to pushing at my throat.

He almost gets a grip on me, but not quite. And then he whispers, soft as rain on grass, "So...smooth..."

As though he's never felt my skin before. I suppose he hasn't. I've certainly never felt him touch me like this. Never felt roughness on the pad of his thumb, never had to submit to such a slow and exploratory caress.

I moan inside.

"You're very beautiful, Margie," he says.

I don't tell him that Roland hasn't called me Margie for years. Instead I let him slide that huge hand up over my throat, and then over my jaw. He cups my face as though I'm made of gold.

I would weep, if it wasn't for all the shaking and the hormones sizzling through my veins with the rushing blood, and the one thought that is in my head: I haven't had sex for two years. My legs are weak. I can feel a second heart beating between my legs, and I don't care who it's beating for.

I turn my face into his hand without a lick of shame. Why would I feel shame when these prickles of electricity are all over me, and his other hand is now finding its way to my shoulder?

He threads his fingers through my hair and I'm sure he's going to pull, but instead he strokes. He draws lines over my scalp and uncovers the jut of bone just below my shoulder. I think about closing my eyes and pretending that he looks different, too.

Even if that's impossible. He's just as handsome as my real husband was, chocolate eyed and firm, intent on me in the same way he used to focus on health and fitness magazines and economic reports. That line is bisecting his forehead, though he isn't frowning. He looks at me with new and wondering eyes, touching me as though I'm unfamiliar.

It isn't hard to touch him back in the same way.

I run my fingers over the taut skin of his stomach, pushing slightly to feel the shape of the muscles beneath. He feels good and new, soft as well as hard, and he murmurs some faint sound for me.

I press my mouth to the well of his navel to make him speak again. Roland never used to speak, but this stranger does. He whispers to me when I poke my tongue in and whispers more as I slide up his body with my mouth leading the way.

Any second he's going to push me down on the bed, any second now. I can feel his erection stiff and insistent against various parts of me, hotter than I feel inside. I'd forgotten how big he is there but I remember now, as my pussy clenches around nothing and I grow slick and desperate for him.

But he makes no real move. His hands pretend that there is no urgency in him, even when I know there is. His cock has twisted out the material of his underwear, and when I turn my head and press my cheek against his hip bone, I can feel the heavy thickness of him like a metal bar laid across the hollow of my throat.

He keeps making those faint noises as he spreads his big hands over my back, never pushing me or bending me into places I don't want to go. With my face turned away I tug at the elastic of his jockeys, not quite getting them down but saying enough with that motion, I think.

I want to kiss his cock. I want to see if he is so different every-where—if those sounds will become something louder, if he'll buck into my mouth and twist on the bed. Will he be hard and forceful, or as tender and teasing as he is now? I feel as though the near nerveless expanse of my back is connected to my cunt, my clit, the tips of my tits. I am aroused by nothing, creaming for his strange evasive touch.

"What do you want, my Margie?" he asks.

I'll beg him, if that's what he'd like. He seems the type to want a little begging, a little squirming. Does he know that I'm squirming inside?

"Are you sure this is what you want?"

I look up at him, hair half in my eyes and my chin to his stomach. I feel the twist of his stiff cock press against my throat again. He looks amused, I think, but darkly intent at the same time. He's just pushing and pushing and waiting for me to—

"Of course this is what I want," I tell him. "You're my husband."

He seems to like that. Those words make his mouth quirk up at the corner, that perfect pink bow of a mouth that I want to kiss more than I ever did back when he was that other Roland. I lick my lips to force him into action but I don't think he's quite ready to give in—not just yet.

Instead he tells me to lie back on the bed—just to see if I will do it, I think.

I do. I do more than that—I spread my legs, too, and show him all of my eagerness. I rifle my nightgown up over my thighs, getting it as high as it will go without it being off altogether. My scent fills the room, musky and sweet and good. Even without that feeling between my legs, of slippery, nerve-rich flesh sliding against even sweeter places, I'd know that I was aroused.

It's in my smell, and in my belly, hot and deep.

I wonder how hot and deep it is in him. He burns more than Roland, I'm certain. He looks calm but he reaches down and grips my thigh so tightly it hurts, but not enough to make me stop this. And when he tugs me down the bed, he puts some effort into getting my thighs as far apart as they will go.

So that he can see the juicy split of my sex, I'm sure. So he can look right down into it as though he's allowed to.

When he strokes me there, I jump and close my eyes. My clit jumps too, right up against his suddenly pressing fingers, and I give him some more juice to make his caress easy. He seems to revel in all the easiness, sliding back and forth through my slit with two eager fingers, and all the time watching, watching, watching.

His eyes burn all over me and then he pushes those fingers down, inside, right into my pussy, while I arch my back up off the bed and grasp for more. *Deeper*, I think, *deeper with those thick, rough fingers*.

But I only think it because I know he's going to tease me some more.

With his free hand he pushes down those clingy little pants, not rushing to get straight between my thighs in order to hide his nakedness. His cock stands close to his belly, gleaming at the tip and as curved and thick and long as I remember—but he's stiffer, redder. He passes his hand over himself only briefly, as though close enough to flashpoint to know he has to take care. His cock bobs all on its own, and a shining thread of precome glistens all the way down the shaft.

I lick my lips again. I'm gripping handfuls of the sheets, and not just because his busy fingers are stirring insistently against that bundle of nerves inside me. He rubs and rubs as though trying to uncover the shape of something.

My body bows under the pressure. I arch my back again and rock my hips up to meet him, one greedy hand lashing out to stop his from moving away when he goes to. He almost smiles, but more than that is the twist and turn of his wet fingers as they leave my pussy and slide over my wrist, freeing him but capturing me.

Now he has hold of my hand, and he wastes no time tugging me to his cock. I grip him eagerly, palm skidding and sliding through all the moisture he's produced just for me. He swells when I squeeze him and I watch his head go back—just a little. Not enough to give himself away.

Though I don't know what *away* he might be giving.

He gives more when I twist on the bed and scramble forward to swallow his heavy flesh down.

His salt-sweet taste is bright against my tongue, but better than that is the feel of him, yielding to the pressure of my mouth until I get to that iron-stiff core. I try out sucks and licks to the beat of his sighing moans, and I'm pushed to work harder when he asks me if I like giving head.

I don't answer him because when I say nothing, he keeps talking. He keeps asking in that wondering tone of voice, as though he can't believe how greedy my mouth is. But of course, it isn't really my mouth that's greedy.

It's my body, and it wants to eat his juddering words. "Oh, god, you feel good," he tells me. "Harder," he tells me. "Hurt me," he tells me.

Instead of obeying I lick the flat of my tongue right over that sweet ridge on the underside, the one that makes him urge himself into my mouth. "I'm going to come, baby," he tells me, and I like that, too.

But I stop short of him going over. I don't want him in my mouth. I want to lie back on the bed and order him, "Mark me."

He knows exactly what I mean. It doesn't take a dozen halting explanations. And he tugs my nightgown down, too, so that my too-tight nipples meet the air. I shiver just to feel that slight caress, but stretch to gather up more of it. I'm vibrating with the need to feel more of it. When he jerks his cock roughly over the bend of my body, thighs caging me in, I shudder all over.

The slit at the tip of his prick opens and closes with each stroke, slipperiness spilling over his fist until I'm sure he's there already. I'm sure until he really does come, the muscles in his thighs tightening and flexing around my body where he's straddling me, his expression so tight and suddenly closed that I imagine it's painful.

It's painful for me waiting, while his spunk stripes my tits and adds another layer of caress. First hot, then cool, then colder yet, icing on the swollen sensitive tips of my breasts.

I shout out loud when he finally comes down from it and runs a curious finger through his cream to spread it around my nipple.

Sparks of sensation radiate through me, but he doesn't let them rest for long. He searches out my aching clit, bending in so strange and sensuous a way. He almost has to reach between his own legs to get to me, and so both the visual and his pressing stroking fingers are the things that send me up.

I struggle against the sudden burst of my orgasm at first, but that only makes it climb higher. It clenches me up tight, my clit swelling into the rough press of his fingers, before letting me go.

I squirm into the mattress, dancing for him in gratitude and bliss, sure that I wouldn't trade anything for this.

I wake in the middle of the night to find him staring at me through the darkness. My skin bristles—I feel it all over me—but I don't move away. I could go to the bathroom or pretend I didn't see him looking—but I don't.

Instead I move forward softly and kiss his mouth in the same way. I kiss it again and then again, but he doesn't take charge like he did earlier. He just lies there, impassively taking what I'm giving out.

I tell him to spread his legs, just as he made me. He has to obey, after all. And he does, pushing the covers down so that I can see his long solid legs spread like a girl's. Roland was always strict about him being a man, and me being a lady; he was always very rigid about it—but this new Roland doesn't seem to care.

He lets me litter his body with bite marks, too. In fact he moans for them and arches into my hot biting mouth, hissing when I catch his spiky nipples and squirming on the bed as I did for him.

He growls when I straddle him and sink down onto his jutting cock. I cage him in, right back. His body feels as big as a mighty pine between my thighs, and even bigger sliding into me. I ache and stretch to accommodate him, sighing when that fat length fills me up.

He sighs too and I actually find my own words: "Talk to me," I tell him, as I work myself on his cock.

"Yes," he replies. "Anytime you want—anything you want."

I squeeze myself tight around him—though I don't have to go far. I'm swollen already from one shivering too-intense orgasm, and he swells inside me at every stroke. When I flutter my pussy around him, he jerks his hips up at me.

I cry out—louder than I ever have done before. I think of the neighbors briefly amidst a miasma of sensation, almost lolling over him and letting him take my hips to dictate the pace, but then I realize with a start that it doesn't matter.

They will only see Roland. They will only hear Roland. They will hear me making love to my husband, again and again and again until I'm raw.

"Is this what you were like before?" he asks between panting breaths, and then quickly afterward—too quickly afterward: "I don't remember you being like this."

But he's too far into this to make any sense anyway and the look on his face forces me not to care. He's frowning and clenching the muscles in his jaw already, sunk deep in my slippery heat and pleased to be there, I think. More than pleased to be there.

He lets out a guttural groan and then a gasp, clutching my hips hard and tugging me onto his jerking cock, but I get there first. I get there first because he pushes my own hand between my thighs and forces me to press the heel of my palm against my clit, and when I do I shake with the strength of it.

I shake until he pulls me down on top of him and kisses words into my hair. "You're not like I remember, Margie."

I think about him saying that the next day, and the day after that, and ever afterward. I think about it when we're in the bathtub together and I soap that strange mark on his shoulder, or when we're watching something together or eating together or as he takes my hand, just as the neighbors stop by for our barbecue dinner.

You're not like I remember, Margie.

I wonder if he has thought about crazy things like body snatchers or pod people or clones, too, though really I haven't thought about any of those things at all. I was scared at first I'll admit, because why would anyone ever do a thing like this? A normal person, I mean. Why would a normal person pretend he was someone else so that he could have lawn chairs and love-making every evening and sometimes in between, and an average job and an average life and all of these things that now seem to make me so happy?

And then I think about his brother. His brother, who I know

had a tattoo on his left shoulder, a tattoo that would probably leave something behind—like a dark mark—if he were to ever have it removed.

Especially if he had it removed somewhere like prison, which is where Roland always said he was.

Of course Roland never spoke much about him at all. Families like his don't talk about bad eggs, who do things like steal and murder and inveigle their way into your secret heart, the secret heart that wants dark instead of light, danger instead of boredom.

But I can't blame Roland for always being the latter any more than I can blame him for never wanting to talk about his brother. It's hard to talk about someone so rotten and wrong, when that wrong and rotten person is your twin.

THE STONE ROOM

A. D. R. Forte

I

James went seeking his fortune. He found it three quarters of the way up a great tower that stretched into the sky. The fortune was fairly abundant as fortunes go and so, as young men are wont to do, he sought adventure next.

He'd been gifted with a well-made sword, one of notable length and girth, and perhaps it was this that made him a little careless. He could venture any challenge, conquer it and leave it later, not worrying that any gentle tendrils might attach themselves to his heart. Every morning, wherever he happened to wake, he cut himself free with ease and went back to making more fortune.

To many a less fortunate adventurer among the great towers, he seemed kissed by Lady Fortune herself. He accepted this without question when others said it. But alone in the castle he'd fashioned of glass and polished wood and expensive knick-knacks within the heart of another tower, he looked out on the realms below and found himself ill at ease.

Sleepless.

Restless.

He searched out ever more conquests, subduing them with ease, but after each he lay awake through the hours of the night, staring into darkness, searching, fretting and thinking that for all he'd won, he'd gained nothing at all.

He had seen the wise woman before. In fact, he saw her every day at the great tower. She looked more girl than woman, perhaps no older than he himself. Thin, mousy, hiding behind thick-rimmed spectacles and plain shirts that hid any shape she might or might not have had. But like him, she could deftly spin gold from nothing but words.

He admired her skill, but beyond that, he had no cause to think of her at all. She had no place in his world beyond the tower walls.

Until he went in search of ever darker adventure.

An acquaintance who knew him better than most, who perhaps guessed at the hidden disquiet in his friend's eyes, told him of the place, invited him to come along one night. *Just to see.*

He went, expecting nothing. It was but another place for the populace to gather and indulge their vices, albeit vices with a strange twist. Like a shallow tourist, he'd be a sore thumb, clearly out of place. But as he sat in a discreet corner with his friend, wineglass in hand, to watch, he felt a cold finger run down his spine.

He chided himself, ashamed that he sought cheap thrills from gawking at the taboo. He had meant to stay collected and detached. He had meant to smile and seem world weary and patronizing.

He left that night with sweat soaking the fine linen of his

shirt beneath his dark jacket, and a hunger like fire in his belly and his loins.

When he slept, he dreamed of pain.

A second time he returned, and then a third time, alone. When his friend could not join him, he secured access for himself. Silent, sober, he watched and dreamed. And so it was the wise woman found him.

Startled at the familiar voice, at the touch on his arm, he turned. For a moment, he didn't recognize the narrow, pointed face between waves of dark hair, or the slender figure in satin and leather. But the smoky eyes behind the spectacles were the same he saw every day in the great tower. He marveled at her presence in this place.

She smiled, something she seldom did at the tower.

"Drew told me he had a friend who would be here tonight. He asked me to take care of you," she explained, voice quiet as ever, but rich with amusement. "I never imagined it would be you of all people."

At that he blushed. Had stories of his conquests reached her? Did she think him here for the same purpose? He wanted to protest his innocence of the crime before she could accuse him, but tongue-tied he could find nothing to say. In the great tower, such things weren't spoken of, weren't even acknowledged to exist, except perhaps in whispers amongst the squares of plastic and fiberglass that dotted the floors. There was nothing he could say.

Silent, he sat with her to watch. And in time the music of blows, of cries, of breath swept him away. He forgot about the tower, forgot the wise woman at his side. Forgot all but the heat in his face and in his loins.

She took his hand and pulled him away from the crowded rooms.

"Come with me. Forget all this," she said. "It's not what you're looking for."

"It's not?" he asked, laughing, recovering a smidgen of his usual poise before she turned and looked at him with huge eyes behind glass that seemed to see right through his rib cage and into his heart.

She shook her head. "No. I don't think so."

A door waited at the bottom of a flight of stairs. They stood halfway down, his hand in hers, and the shadows of the stairwell seemed to wrap themselves around her, tangling in her unruly hair and the trailing sleeves of her blouse. He had consumed not a drop of alcohol, but his head still spun, weightless as a balloon.

I can give you what you want. Your body's desire. Your heart's desire.

Did she say it? Or did he conjure the words out of wishful thinking and put them into her unassuming, serene voice.

"Okay," he said.

She opened the door for him.

A giant waited on the other side, as if he'd been expecting them. Behind his broad shoulders, stark walls of stone lit by pale blue-white light waited. The smell of antiseptic and leather mingled in the cool air.

"This is James," she told the giant.

He started at the sound of his name in this place, though he could not imagine why. He feared nothing. He had seen everything there was to see, could conquer anything, and nothing ever held him long before he wriggled free and went on, searching. Why then should this be any different?

The giant nodded acknowledgment and spoke but one word. "Welcome."

Bands of thick leather crossed the man's arms beneath the rolled up sleeves of his shirt. His eyes were shards of blue ice, his head shaved smooth, and James had to tilt his own gaze up ever so slightly to meet the giant's. But James's own arms were as muscled, his shoulders as broad, and he didn't fear.

He could pass their test.

As for his heart's desire, he wouldn't think of that. Not now. And how could he, when he had no inkling of what it might even be?

They stripped him of his clothing and shackled his hands above his head, locked his bare feet to either end of an iron bar that kept his legs spread wide. He said not a word, made not a sound.

Bear it without complaint or resistance, she had told him. If he protested, they would stop. They would send him back to the world above, and he would be safe, unhurt, unblemished...and he would have failed.

He refused to fail.

At the first vicious kiss of the leather, he closed his eyes and took a deep breath as the giant had warned him he must do, but the breath still froze in his throat. Stinging lines snaked down his back and his ass. Even knowing it was unwise, he could not help his muscles from tensing against the threat of pain, and the next sting wrung a stifled cry from his lips.

Between his legs need stirred, kindled by the insistent brutal force that had filled his dreams with images of welted skin and straining limbs for days, for weeks without number now. The lashes came faster, then slower, driven by the force of the giant's powerful arm, and their bite turned fiery.

Despite the chill of the stone, perspiration trickled down his skin and he feared he would lose his balance, his legs trembled so. But he squeezed his hands into fists and gritted his teeth, held on while the blood pounded in his temples. And with each new blow the hunger crested and ebbed, tormented him beyond endurance. It urged him to scream, to beg for release, to demand anything but this silent helplessness.

First a pause. Then another tongue of fire down his inflamed skin. Then another rasping breath in his raw throat, dry as bone. An endless cycle.

Head spinning, he imagined his body dissolving: lava and brimstone. Somewhere, beyond consciousness, blinking sweat and tears from his eyes, he stared up at the stone ceiling, at white-blue light, and knew the whip had stopped.

Ah, but it was too late, part of his mind whispered. *Too late*. He knew he could not fight what would be inevitable now.

The giant's hot mouth closed around his taut flesh and a low, guttural moan broke from him, in a voice he barely recognized as his own. He felt the rough brush of moustache and beard on his skin, and sweet tingles danced like imps through his blood. He moaned.

This was a trial to be endured and survived. He should not enjoy it, should not want it…but then never had he imagined such a thing. Never would he have approved of it even if he had. He twisted his head from side to side, as if he might shake the thoughts out of it.

But he would not cry out now. He would not fail. He could not.

He desired that mouth, and the broad, rough hands that caressed his welted back and his balls; the throat that swallowed the length of his blade with knowing expertise; the strong hands that held him still as he bucked and writhed and surrendered at last with a meaningless scream.

Lava unleashed. Molten.

II
He awoke in his own bed, with the memory of his night in the stone room as raw as his skin. His hands moved to touch the

sheathed blade that had betrayed him so spectacularly, and he tensed again at the remembrance. Blissful agony.

"I will call you," the wise woman had said, her gaze hidden behind the tangle of dark hair as she led him up the stairs and left him to find his way through rooms that passed in a blur to the night outside.

He understood. One night only was not enough for the enchantment. It demanded he abandon every shred of self, every trace of pride, all pretense of control.

Curled among cool sheets with his arms about a pillow of softest goose feathers encased in the finest Egyptian cotton, he knew at last what he feared.

When he returned to the room of stone, the giant bound a cloth of black over his eyes and cuffed his hands and his throat. The giant and the wise woman snapped teeth of steel into his flesh: his nipples, the skin of his balls. He gasped, and they forced a ball of rubber between his lips before they took him, blind and bare, up the stairs and away, some far distance that he could neither see nor measure, and into the heat of a crowded place.

Here, exclamations of surprise and delight greeted him. Hands pulled at him, pinched and tugged and twisted until his flesh hurt in a hundred places. The ball was taken from his mouth and unseen mouths kissed his, laughing. Invisible hands slapped his bare ass, jiggled the cruel clips in his flesh.

They made him kneel and his mouth served them: men and women, hard as stone, soft as silk.

Oh. What a lovely toy.

Wherever did you find him?

They whipped him again and broke his skin with their nails, but he suffered it all with not a word, until his stiff, aching body could scarcely move. Without thinking, he followed the lead of the hand that guided him to the depths of a soft bed. Through blurry, throbbing eyes he saw the face of the wise woman as she lifted the cloth from his eyes.

Exhausted, he slept the dreamless sleep of the used.

He did not return to his home when he woke again. The wise woman came to find him and once more he stared in surprise, for though the spectacles perched on her nose, her hair fell in a long, soft twist over one shoulder and where light shone through the pure, white linen of her clothing he saw the naked curves of her body.

"Rise and bathe," she ordered him, and he did as she said, in her bath of pale, green marble. He went to her afterward with his wet hair still dripping on his naked shoulders, and she smiled with approval.

She asked a silent question with her eyes that reminded him of storm clouds. He nodded in reply.

For the third time he let her bind his hands above his head as he lay with his face in yielding pillows that smelled of her: like rain and summer. He closed his eyes, and she parted his legs, and he thought, *I cannot bear this.*

For he could feel lines like spider silk weaving themselves about his heart as her fingers toyed with his flesh. She opened him with her touch and then her kiss, and he shuddered as her tongue slid into him, moved inside him.

The muscles of his stomach quivered, jellylike, as if they might turn to liquid. His hips moved involuntarily, but she stilled him with a touch.

She whispered words he did not hear. He understood all the same.

Her hair fell loose across his back, and her hands gripped his shoulders. Beneath her he held his breath, and her sword, one of rubber and of leather, pierced him. Heat ran through his body, set him shivering. Still sore and bruised, maddened by this new pleasure that masqueraded as pain, he gripped the sheets in his fist and resisted her. Fought her. And found it brought him ever more delight.

She laughed and flung her slender arms about his shoulders, rested her cheek on his back while her hips moved against his ass. She ravished him. Broke him.

Thus she cast her spell.

III

After that, James belonged to the wise woman, his enchantress in disguise. With her smile and her hair like night, and her eyes the color of smoke and cloud, she had bewitched him utterly.

She kept his heart fast, bound with brambles that made him bleed and sigh. In turn he brought his sword to serve her better and more skillfully than ever he'd served anyone in his life. From time to time, she took him to some grand place hung with chandeliers and curtains of gold where she might offer him up as a toy. Or she brought him back to the stone room where the giant was always pleased to see him.

But ever and always, James knew he was *hers,* and it made his joy complete.

Nor did he seek any more adventures, for indeed, much more might have killed him. And what need had he of adventure when he had found bliss?

So James and the enchantress lived happily ever after, in contentment of a strange and wonderful kind, for all the rest of their days.

ABOUT THE AUTHORS

JANINE ASHBLESS (janineashbless.blogspot.com) has two collections of erotic fairy, fantasy and paranormal stories, *Cruel Enchantment* and *Dark Enchantment*. She was *Jade* magazine's Erotic Fiction Writer of the Year 2009. Her short stories have appeared in several Cleis anthologies including *Best Women's Erotica 2009*.

MICHELLE AUGELLO-PAGE is a writer living in New York. She received an MFA from Adelphi University and is a teacher in an alternative elementary school. Recent poetry has been published in *The Mom Egg*, *Mannequin Envy* and *Copper Nickel*; recent fiction has been published in *Tales from the Moonlit Path*.

ANDREA DALE's (cyvarwydd.com) stories have appeared in *Alison's Wonderland*, *The Sweetest Kiss* and *Lesbian Cowboys*, among many others. With coauthors, she has sold two novels to Virgin Books. She loves all things fantastical and believes fairy tales should be for grown-ups.

DELILAH DEVLIN (DelilahDevlin.com) is an author of erotic romance with a rapidly expanding reputation for writing deliciously edgy stories with complex characters, whether creating dark, erotically charged paranormal worlds or richly descriptive westerns that ring with authenticity.

JEREMY EDWARDS (jeremyedwardserotica.com) is the author of the erotocomedic novel *Rock My Socks Off*. His short stories have appeared in over forty anthologies, including three volumes in the *Mammoth Book of Best New Erotica* series.

JUSTINE ELYOT's short fiction has appeared in numerous anthologies, as well as in her single-author collection, *On Demand*. She lives in the United Kingdom, by the sea.

AURELIA T. EVANS (aureliatevans@yahoo.com) graduated from Trinity University in May 2008. She now works as a communications assistant by day and writer by night. Her short story "In Circles" was published in the queer erotic horror anthology *Kiss of the Spider Woman*.

A. D. R. FORTE (adrforte.blogspot.com) is the author of erotic short fiction that appears in numerous anthologies, including the acclaimed *Best Women's Erotica*. Her tales of erotic fantasy can be found in collections from Cleis Press and Circlet Press.

SHANNA GERMAIN (shannagermain.com) is careful to keep her hem dry and her hands away from blocks of salted cream. Her work has appeared in places like *Best American Erotica*, *Best Gay Bondage*, *Best Gay Romance*, *Best Lesbian Erotica*, *Please, Sir* and more.

LOUISA HARTE (louisaharte.com) loves crafting erotic and romantic fiction. Her work features in the anthology *Best Women's Erotica 2010*. Currently living in New Zealand, she finds inspiration from many places, including her thoughts, dreams and fantasies.

CAROL HASSLER (halcyonflow@gmail.com) is a mild-mannered librarian by day and a caffeine-fueled writer by night. Fairy tales often inspire her work, which ranges from fantasy to science fiction (with a little horror thrown in the mix). Carol enjoys baking but has never actually made a live man.

ANGELA KNIGHT (angelasknights.com) is the *New York Times* bestselling author of *Guardian* and other novels. Besides her fiction work, Angela's publishing career includes a stint as a comic book writer and ten years as a newspaper reporter. Several of her stories won South Carolina Press Association awards under her real name. Angela's newest novel is *Master of Fire*.

CRAIG SORENSEN (just-craig.blogspot.com) believes in the happily ever afterlife. His stories have appeared in numerous print anthologies and magazines as well as online.

CHARLOTTE STEIN (themightycharlottestein.blogspot.com) has published a number of stories in various erotic anthologies, including *Sexy Little Numbers*. She is also the author of the short-story collection *The Things That Make Me Give In* and a novella, *Waiting In Vain*.

ALEGRA VERDE (litprofessor@hotmail.com) lives in the Midwest where she tries to find time to finish her first novel while teaching literature at the local college. Her most recent erotic fiction can be found in the anthologies *Misbehavior* and *The Affair*.

When **ALANA NOËL VOTH** isn't working a day job or taking care of her kiddo, she's writing. Her work has appeared in *Best Women's Erotica*, *Best Gay Erotica* and *The Mammoth Book of Best New Erotica*. Her story "Genuflection" was selected for *Best American Erotica 2005*.

SASKIA WALKER (saskiawalker.co.uk) is a British author whose short fiction appears in numerous anthologies. Her erotic novels include *Along for the Ride*, *Double Dare*, *Reckless*, *Rampant* and *Inescapable*. Saskia lives in the north of England close to the windswept Yorkshire moors, where she happily spends her days spinning yarns.

ALLISON WONDERLAND (aisforallison.blogspot.com) has been writing erotica since 2007. She's contributed to *Coming Together*, *Best Lesbian Erotica 2010* and *Alison's Wonderland*, among others. Aside from erotica, Allison's indulgences include cotton candy, kitten heels and Old Hollywood glamour.

ABOUT THE EDITOR

KRISTINA WRIGHT (kristinawright.com) is an author, editor and college instructor. Her erotica and erotic romance fiction have appeared in over seventy-five print anthologies, including *Bedding Down: A Collection of Winter Erotica*; *Dirty Girls: Erotica for Women*; *Sweet Love: Erotic Fantasies for Couples*; three editions of *Best Women's Erotica*; four editions of *Best Lesbian Erotica*; five editions of the *Mammoth Book of Best New Erotica* and the erotic romance collections *Seduction*, *Liaisons* and *Sexy Little Numbers*. She received the Golden Heart Award for Romantic Suspense from Romance Writers of America for her first novel *Dangerous Curves*, which was published by Silhouette Books. Her work has also been featured in the nonfiction guide *The Many Joys of Sex Toys* and magazines and e-zines such as Clean Sheets, Good Vibes Magazine, *Libida*, *The Fiction Writer*, *The Literary Times*, Scarlet Letters, *The Sun* and *The Quill*. Her essay "The Last Letter" is included in the epistolary anthology *P.S. What I Didn't Say: Unsent Letters to Our*

Female Friends and her articles, interviews and book reviews have appeared in numerous publications, both print and online. She is a member of Romance Writers of America, Passionate Ink and the Erotica Readers and Writers Association. She holds degrees in English and humanities and teaches English composition and world mythology at the community college level. Originally from South Florida, Kristina has lived up and down the East Coast with her husband, Jay, a naval officer. They now call Virginia home and recently welcomed the addition of their son Patrick, born in December 2009.